CAGE ME

A DRAGONS LOVE CURVES NOVEL

AIDY AWARD

Copyright © 2018 by Aidy Award.

All rights reserved. No part of this publication may be reproduced, distributed or transmitted in any form or by any means, including photocopying, recording, or other electronic or mechanical methods, without the prior written permission of the publisher, except in the case of brief quotations embodied in critical reviews and certain other noncommercial uses permitted by copyright law. For permission requests, write to the publisher, addressed "Attention: Permissions Coordinator," at the address below.

Aidy Award/Coffee Break Publishing

www.coffeebreakpublishing.com

Publisher's Note: This is a work of fiction. Names, characters, places, and incidents are a product of the author's imagination. Locales and public names are sometimes used for atmospheric purposes. Any resemblance to actual people, living or dead, or to businesses, companies, events, institutions, or locales is completely coincidental.

Cover Design by Melody Simmons

Cage Me/ Aidy Award. -- 1st ed.

ISBN-13: 978-1-950228-50-8

❀ Created with Vellum

For Uno ~ my love.

Because he doesn't do anything to earn any money to pay rent, never does the dishes when I ask him to, sits in my lap when I write, and lets me snuggle him real hard when I cry.

ACKNOWLEDGMENTS

I want to thank my two proofreaders, Corinne and Hopey. I am totally sending you both signed copies of this book. All the mistakes left are my own.

And as to the Amazeballs – you all are exactly that.

Thanks to those of you that told me it was okay to take care of me when Cage was trying to kill me, told your friends all about the dragons series, and were so damned excited for this book to come out. You all are why I write.

Hugs,

--A

A fish and a bird can fall in love,
but where would they live?

—Someone pessimistic

NEVER SAY DIE

*H*e would not quit.

He would not let his people down, nor his mate. The warrior inside of him would never allow it.

Cage threw a punch, ducked and weaved, then threw another. He might not be able to shift into his dragon form anymore, but he could still fight.

He growled at his opponent who treated him like a little fucking flower. "Come on, Zon. Bring it. Don't go easy on me. My bare knuckles are all I've got left to fight with. I'm not quitting until they're bruised and bloody."

If he had to die trying, he would ensure the future of the gold dragons.

His sparring partner lunged and caught Cage right on the jaw, snapping his head back. He tumbled to the floor and spit out the blood pooling in his mouth. Served him right for navel-gazing. Warriors didn't think, they didn't screw around.

About time he learned that lesson.

Better late than never.

Probably.

"Sorry, sir." Zon looked down, the telltale worry in eyes. God, how Cage was tired of concerned looks. He'd lost his dragon, but it didn't make him a breakable baby.

He waved the offered hand away. "I'm fine. But remind me to dock your pay later."

That anxious look turned to shock. Thank the First Dragon, because one more second of being pitied and Cage really would start docking warriors' pay.

That would teach them. Gold dragon warriors were greedy bastards.

"Kidding, man. Teach me that move and I just might give you the key to my lair."

Another look of shock. Cage really needed to get his men to lighten up.

Worry was not the way to be a warrior. Action was.

AmberGris, his second in command, and Zon's twin walked into the training room and frowned at Cage lying on the floor. He assessed the situation, folded his arms, not pleased, and scowled at Zon, who shrugged.

The two exchanged glances that had a whole lot of – what the hell is going on here – I don't know, he asked me to spar with him – well, you have to be careful with him, he's weak – communication between them. Before Cage could smack them both upside the head, Gris gave him the news he'd been waiting for.

"Sir, we have her."

Cage ignored everything else and pulled himself up from the mats. "Good work. Put her in my office and draw the shades. We want to make our guest as comfortable as possible."

"Respectfully, sir, she's been a giant pain in the ass and I would prefer we escort her to the dungeon where I – we - can keep a better eye on her."

Gris was an excellent dragon warrior… and a little overdramatic. Cage had turned The Lindens' dungeon into a wine cellar years ago. But, since this whole shit storm had started, Gris had become an overprotective mother hen.

"I'm sure you would. Put her in my office anyway."

Gris grumbled, and Cage could practically see his feathers puffing up. "Sir."

Cage raised up a hand to hold the oncoming objections. "I promise you and the rest of the guard won't be far away when I question her. She's already stolen my soul shard once. It's not like she can get it again."

Cage waved to his empty chest. It still felt strange to not be wearing the talisman that held a piece of his soul intermingled with the First Dragon's.

She'd stolen a whole hell of a lot more from him than his shard, she'd taken something precious from every Golden Dragon.

And it was his own damn fault.

Gris huffed and puffed, stirring up small dust devils, but went back to his duties. Probably going to put about twenty more dragons on patrol around the little succubus.

Cage couldn't blame him, and if worse came to really fucking worst, Gris would make a good Wyvern. Not that he wanted the job, but if Cage didn't accomplish this mission, well, let's just say he'd plan the coup himself.

There is only one way Cage could be the true Wyvern his golds needed. That was to get his dragon back. There was only one way to do that.

Go to hell and find his mate.

There was a lot more riding on Cage finding his mate than just his own forsaken soul. The souls of the rest of his Wyr and all their potential mates depended on it.

No pressure.

Jakob and Ky, Wyverns of two of the other dragon Wyrs had already found their mates. The first in centuries. None of them had even thought it was a possibility.

Since then, in just a few short weeks, at least a dozen more dragons had found, marked, claimed, and mated women who filled their souls and their powers to overflowing. But, only Jakob's greens and Ky's blue dragons had been blessed.

The reds and his own golds were just fucked.

The AllWyr council had surmised that the Wyvern of each Wyr must have to be mated before the rest of his dragons would be able to.

The only thing keeping Cage from going berserk and killing every demon dragon under the sun was the fact that he already knew who she was.

Azynsa.

Such a strange and beautiful name.

It was almost all he knew about her. That and she was half mermaid.

The fates had to be laughing their asses off for coming up with that one. A flyer of the skies and a lush creature of the ocean, soul mates.

Where in the world would they live?

He'd figure that out later, assuming they both survived long enough to get together.

Azynsa already owned his soul.

Quite literally.

He'd known it the instant she'd touched his missing soul shard. She'd healed him from the worst case of man-flu in the universe. Even though they'd been on different planes, separated by miles, space, and time, he knew her and their connection.

Weirdest fucking feeling ever. Like a miracle wrapped up in an enigma sprinkled with fear and fairy dust.

Azynsa was his true mate, and he was hers.

Only problem, she'd been kidnapped by the Black Dragon, the king of hell, and when his brother Wyverns had tried to save her, she'd… disappeared.

Ky and Jakob had left her on the promise from some shithead of a rogue dragon, that she too had escaped.

He knew better.

She was down there. Tortured by the heat and something that weighed heavy on her heart. He'd had dreams of her hiding, spying, crying.

No, not crying. She had yet to shed a tear.

The dreams were not his imagination. He suffered her pain and sorrow as if he were there with her. A part of him was.

He'd also known her bravery, an internal toughness that even most dragon warriors couldn't match.

She was one badass mermaid.

Every waking hour he plotted and planned, trained his human body to fight and survive, all so he could rescue her from the pits of hell.

He had a strategy to get a guide to hell. Once he got down there he'd have to survive without his dragon in a realm filled with demons, demon dragons, the Black Dragon, and no possibility of sunshine, to recharge him, ever.

None of the dangers mattered, not if they meant he could rescue Azynsa and lift whatever spell was keeping his Wyr from finding their mates.

Cage headed to the main house and stretched out while crossing the garden, basking in the direct rays of the sun. He really ought to live on a beach somewhere, but Denmark and The Lindens estate had been the Gold Wyr seat for longer than he could remember. Besides, a big chunk of his treasure hoard was here. It would be a giant pain to move, and how did one hide billions of dollars of gold, art, gold, jewels, and more gold in the sand?

He got plenty of sunshine here and when the skies were gray and cloudy, all he had to do was fly above them to refill his energy.

Except he couldn't do that anymore.

He couldn't live without the sun and not just because he needed to work on his tan. Which meant hell…would be hell.

He was going there anyway.

He'd already decided not to ask Jakob or Ky to join this battle. It wasn't fair to them or their new mates to ask them to put themselves at risk again. Match was the perfect choice to go with. That bastard loved the dark and heat of a volcano. But, he was still recovering from a dagger to the heart, poisoned with something that had almost killed him.

He'd be grumpy the whole time anyway. He was always grumpy.

Time to get creative.

Actually, he already had.

He closed his eyes and lifted his face to the sun, for one more minute of its energy. He had a feeling he would need all he could get.

When he got back to the house, two of his gold warriors were standing guard at the entrance to his office.

Behind the closed doors someone swore like a sailor who was raised by swearing sailors.

He'd always had a thing for filthy mouths.

"You two can go. I don't think you need to hear this."

They nodded and saluted and then stood there like statues. They weren't going anywhere. None of his guard had let him alone for a month. Either that or the succubus allure had them constrained.

He scowled at them and they didn't even flinch.

Fine, it was their dicks.

He pushed through the door and it took his eyes a minute to adjust to the dark room. All of the curtains had been drawn and the lights were off.

"Don't you come a fucking step closer to me, Cage. I have no intention of dying today."

Cage found his little thief stuffed into the corner of the room, hiding behind his desk. She had a letter opener in her hand, ready to use like a knife. There was a lot of bravado in her words, but the tremor behind them betrayed her fear.

She should be afraid.

"Hello, Portia. Stole any other souls lately?"

He knew full well she hadn't done anything besides run for the past few weeks. She'd been excommunicated from every demon coven in the world. She had to be scared, lonely, and hungry. Exactly how he wanted her.

"Screw you, you gave it to me."

That tough exterior had been what attracted him to her in the first place. That and her allure. Which she wasn't using now. Interesting. Cage's eyes adjusted to the dark and he sauntered toward Portia. "We've already done the screwing part, my dear."

She held the letter opener at the ready, and she knew how to wield it too. Leonard had taught her to fight. It was probably the only reason she was still alive. Succubae did not do well on their own.

"I'm not apologizing for all that. I did what I thought I had to do."

He wasn't blaming her, never had. It was his own damn fault for getting involved with a succubus in the first place. Well, it was his dick's fault.

He liked sex just as much as the next dragon, maybe more. Who better at sex than a succubus?

But truth be told, he hadn't been that into it lately. He figured it was just his Prime coming on. Dragons from his generation and the one before him, were well known to be horny little fucks in their younger days, but when they hit around a hundred and fifty and their aging slowed down, so did their libidos. He wasn't really ready to throw in the towel, like Match had.

That guy needed to get laid more than anyone he knew.

Cage's latest partners hadn't been disappointed. He knew how to make a woman come, screaming his name. He hadn't got off himself in months.

Portia's allure had gotten a rise out of him though. She'd worked her mojo and he'd welcomed it, with open pants.

He'd been so under her spell, that she could have asked for the moon, and he would've flown up to give it to her. But all she asked him for was his soul shard.

Even while he handed it over to her he knew it was a horrible idea. But, she'd controlled him completely.

Not today.

Cage flipped on the light switch, keeping her as off balance as he could. She preferred the dark.

He preferred to have a soul.

She squeaked and dove under the desk.

"I'm not here to eat you, Portia." Although she probably would've liked it. "I'm calling in the favor you owe me."

"I don't owe you shit." Her voice came up from her hiding place.

Cage laughed darkly. That was the most hilarious and horrible thing he'd ever heard. "Oh, I think you do. You owe me a whole lot more than that. But, I've got a deal for you. Do what I ask, and I have something for you in return."

He kept his tone seductive, doing his best to speak her language. Portia and what was inside her head were his best and only plan to get to hell and back.

"If that something involves chopping off my head, I'll pass, and also, fuck you."

"I hear you're homeless, without a coven. Not a friend in the world. Wouldn't it be nice to have someone on your side again, Portia?"

She gripped the edge of the desk and her face slowly rose above it. "What are you offering?"

Gotcha.

"You help me find my mate, and you can live here, under my protection. We'll find a way to feed you in any way you might need."

It wouldn't take much of her allure to get most of his dragons to fuck and feed her. Except maybe Gris. He had a particular hard-on for Portia, and not the fun kind.

Portia's face went paler than usual and sunk back down below eye level of the desk. "Why would you do that for me?"

Cage leaned against the desk and crossed one leg over the other as if none of this mattered to him one bit. "You have the key to getting me down to hell."

"Oh no. I'm not going back there."

He needed to entice her a little bit more. "I can provide you with everything your coven ever did and more."

"I doubt that. Leonard and Geshtianna are very old demons. They're a lot more powerful than you or any of your dragon buddies."

Yes, but he had a trump card. "Maybe, but I can give you something they can't."

Portia was playing tough, but Cage knew he had her hooked. Her incubus father was powerful, but he'd also banished her. She had nothing, and he was about to offer her everything.

Cage waited patiently for her mind to come to the conclusion all on her own that she had no other choice. Regardless of what he had for her, it was a better option than life on her own. She knew it and so did he.

He could throw her in the dungeon and feed her on rats and she'd take it. Lucky for her he was offering something much better.

"What do you want from me? I can't take you down there. I was just along for the ride and lost everything while your dragons were off saving the day. Go ask them to help you."

"They've done enough. Besides, they don't have what you do." He had no intention of taking Portia back down into hell. She wouldn't be able to help him. Only one dragon could do that.

"Quit dicking me around and tell me what you want. My allure might not work on you or your golden retriever, but I'm pretty sure those two at the door are ready to come in here and fight you for me."

This sparring was the most fun he'd had in weeks. At least Portia didn't treat him like everyone else in his life at the moment. They were both vulnerable and that put them on an equal footing. "Why is it you haven't just turned your allure on me again? We both know you could simply make me tell you my plans and take whatever you want in the process."

"Yeah, like I haven't tried?"

He hadn't felt a thing.

Portia sighed. "Jada says our allure doesn't work on dragons who are mated, you bastard."

That may be true, but it wasn't why she didn't have any power over him. If he was mated, then the rest of his dragons would be finding their mates too. He was in a weird half-mated limbo.

She hadn't been able to dissuade Gris from his task of capturing her either. Her allure must be on the fritz from not having fed. The human side of her was probably the only thing keeping her alive.

Once their deal was done he'd have Gris bring her a nice big meal of human food. If she wanted or needed more than that, he'd feed her himself if he had to. But, only blood this time.

Cage had drawn this game out with Portia long enough. She was desperate already, but now that he'd dangled a safe future in front of her, she'd be ready to give him the one person he needed, betrayal or not.

"I've got the money and resources to give you everything you need. All you have to do is help me with one thing."

"Like I have a choice?"

"We always have choices, babe. We don't always make the smart ones though. I'm proof of that, aren't I?"

Portia crawled out from under the desk and stood, the letter opener still gripped in her hand, but finally she faced him. "What do you want?"

"Your boyfriend."

She frowned and held out the letter opener. "Fuck off. Jett's not mine to give. Never was."

Yeah, and that black dragon bastard never should have let her think otherwise. But he had started this and Cage was going to finish it. "But, you'll find a way to get him here and get him to do what I want anyway."

She bit her lip and shook her head. "I don't know if I can."

"You'll find a way, because once he and I retrieve my mate," that was the plan, "you'll get yours."

She backed away. "Get my what?"

"Your mate, Portia." Boom.

"I don't think it was a coincidence you came to me to get a soul shard. Your mate is a gold dragon. Once I claim Azynsa, your mate will be able to claim you."

Portia dropped down into the chair, shock and awe on her face. Cage knew the feeling.

"Jett is going to kill me for this."

Not if Cage got to kill Jett first. But only after they went to hell and back.

JUST ANOTHER DAY IN HELL

*M*ermaids had been hiding from people for centuries and her mother's people, the Mami Wata, had taught Azynsa some brilliant techniques in the past couple of years for evading prying eyes. For two weeks, or what she guesstimated was about that long, she'd used every damn trick they'd taught her, plus the ones she'd learned growing up, in order to stay alive.

These demon dragons searching for her weren't any worse than the gang bangers in her old neighborhood in Chicago. They were definitely as dumb and as easily manipulated by power and violence. She'd seen that firsthand. Back then and right now.

The Black Dragon chopped off the head of another demon dragon with a flick of its tail while Azy watched incognito. It too disintegrated into a pile of black ash like the three before it. Then the Black Dragon shifted back into its human form, a darkly evil man on a mission. Kur-Jara, the king of hell. "The rest of you find that girl or I'll slice each and every one of your heads from your worthless bodies."

Yeah. She was that girl.

The demon dragons scattered and Azy shrunk back into the

hidey hole she'd climbed into a few hours before. The light from the pools of lava didn't quite reach up here and her dark skin helped her to blend in. The only thing that could give away her position was the light that continued to sparkle in the crystal she wore around her neck.

She would never take it off. It was the only thing keeping her alive down here. That and her street smarts. Every time she grasped the shard in her hand, which was pretty much constantly so it's light wouldn't be visible, a sense of hope filled her, kept her going.

Without it she would have given up days ago.

"They won't find her, father." The woman's voice carried up through the rocks and directly into Azy's ears. "She's not here."

That woman and the sacrifice she'd made for Azynsa was her sole reason for staying in this literal hell hole.

"Fallyn, my little red devil. You said she was." His tone was like an irritated parent trying to get a recalcitrant child to tell him where she'd hidden his car keys.

Azy had done that once, with the keys to her father's police cruiser. Even threats that he'd put her in jail, which she'd believed at the time he could do, didn't convince her to give them back.

Fallyn was no child. She was over a hundred and fifty years old but looked like she was only a few years older than Azy's twenty-three years.

The scars on Fallyn's back from Kur-Jara's fire whip were the only mar on her beautiful curvy body.

Fallyn tipped her head to the side as if thinking. "She is."

"Which is it?" Kur-Jara growled.

Fallyn glanced up and looked Azy straight in the eye. The hot air in the cavern evaporated, or maybe Azy forgot to take another breath. Would Fallyn finally give her away, betray her after all?

"Both. Neither. She's here. But she isn't."

Another much older woman joined them. She was the one to be afraid of. A black witch, *the* Black Witch.

She scanned the area but didn't spot Azy, even though she'd looked right into the hiding spot, just the same as Fallyn did. The witch crossed to Fallyn, throwing a glare at Kur-Jara and wrapped an arm around her.

"Child, use your gift for me to tell us where she is. You know how important it is that we find her. She could be the key to making those horrible dragon warriors pay for everything they have done to us. You want that, don't you?"

Fallyn blinked and frowned. "It doesn't work that way with her. She's here and there. Mated and not."

Kur-Jara growled and stomped around the small cavern. Such a whiny bitch.

"That's why we need her, dammit. If we control her, we control her dragon. I want that soul."

Fallyn shrugged, not intimidated by Kur-Jara even a little. "I could tell you where she is. But she isn't there."

Even Azy wasn't sure at this point whether Fallyn was friend or foe, lying, playing games, or just damn crazy-pants.

Azy would be a slobbering mess, sporting a straitjacket, chilling in her padded room, if she'd been raised by these two fucktards. Her money was on that Fallyn was completely insane, like we're talking Harley Quinn obsessed with the Joker cuckoo for Cocoa Puffs insane.

And it was partly Azy's fault.

"Talk some sense into her, crone. She does what you want. Brat." He snarled at Fallyn but didn't strike her. She was the only one who he seemed to be able to control his violence toward. Even the Black Witch wasn't safe from his rages.

"Then send some of your Annunaki to my chamber. I need to fuck at least three of four of them to work off my frustration over this bitch of a mermaid and," he glanced at the black stains on the floor, "my army is dwindling." Kur-Jara stomped off.

Jesus, Mary and Joseph and all his carpenter friends. The things she'd seen and heard down here, skulking around and trying to stay hidden. If she ever escaped, she should write a book.

God, she missed books.

Not that anyone would believe a word. Azy couldn't imagine being made to have sex with that asshole, much less bear his demon spawn only to have them become pawns in his deadly game with the dragons.

The Annunaki demons didn't seem to care either way. They didn't give a fudge about anything but what the witch told them to do. Then they did it. Had to be under one of the Black Witch's spells, like the demon dragons.

Azy sure as shit wished she didn't know anything about the inner workings of hell. She'd only just gotten used to the bizarro world of the Mami Wata. Five years ago, she hadn't known anything about mermaids, dragons, witches, demons, or any other paranormal being except what she'd read in romance novels. Now the human world seemed a million miles away, getting further every minute.

Honestly, at this point she'd take the dumbass dragons and the xenophobic mermaids over this hellhole. That was a sentence she thought she'd never say in her life.

Damn, she really needed to get out of here.

She would, she had to believe that. But, in all of her observations - spying really - she hadn't found a single shred she could use to convince Fallyn to leave with her.

It was the reason she had taken this risk in hiding almost in plain sight here in the main cavern. She'd almost blown her cover and still hadn't learned anything new. Except that even under direct questioning, Fallyn hadn't given her away. Azy's debts to the woman just kept piling up. Maybe, just maybe, it meant Fallyn felt the tiniest bit of loyalty toward her.

Better than the blind, brainwashed woman she'd spoken with a few days, or maybe it was a whole week, ago.

Each time they met and Azy thought she was making headway, the Black Witch would undo it all. One step forward, two steps back in a macabre dance for Fallyn's life.

The old witch and Fallyn didn't leave the cavern after Kur-Jara threw his fit. Normally, Azy stayed as far away from the Black Witch as she could. Hiding and kicking demon's asses was one thing. There was no defense against dark magical spells.

She rarely heard what kind of manipulative information the crone said to Fallyn. If she was very lucky, maybe they would stay where she could see and hear them and Azy would get a head start on damage control.

Because the witch hadn't seen her, and Fallyn didn't reveal her location, Azy crept forward along the high wall to get closer. Her big ole thighs kept a tight grip on the rocks as she crawled along them. She'd lost a lot more weight in the past two weeks than any other time in her life. But honestly, she did not recommend the demon diet.

As soon as she got out of here she was getting a tray of fully loaded Chicago dogs, a crap ton of greasy French fries, and an entire banana cream pie. She was not sharing any of it with anyone. When she had eaten her fill, she was getting a blender and a bottle of tequila and drinking margaritas in a swimming pool for at least three days.

That day was not today. If she ever expected to get out of here she needed to keep her head in the game, not at Portillo's.

A few tiny pebbles scattered when she hit a patch of loose rocks with her knees. She froze and waited to see if anyone noticed.

"You are not trying hard enough, girl. How will we ever be safe from the dragons if you won't try?"

Oh, yeah. The crone was laying it on thick. Azy had seen enough manipulative losers do the same thing to women back home. Women who should have been smart, savvy, and sexy were turned into quiet idiots with zero self-confidence all in the name of having a man.

Was that same promise of love what kept Fallyn from seeing the truth about the hell she lived in?

"I'm sorry. I'll try harder."

"Good girl. You wouldn't want to make me have to send you to Geshtianna, would you?"

Fallyn jerked her chin almost as if she'd been struck. This Geshtianna chick must be bad news if Fallyn was afraid of her."

"No. Don't. I don't like her, what she or Dumuzid do."

"I don't want to, child. But, Tianna helps us. She never says she can't. Not like you. She's grateful for what I've given her."

Nobody should be happy the Black Witch ever gave them anything. Except complete psychopaths probably would love to cozy up to someone this powerful. Azy's guess was that whoever Geshtianna and Dumuzid were, they were besties with the likes of Bundy, Dahmer, and Lizzie Borden.

The Black Witch *tsked* and folded her arms, withdrawing. "If you don't find the mate, it won't be my fault if she has to use her bite to get what we need from you."

Fallyn put her hand to her neck.

Dear God. Enough was enough. Azy had hidden and spied, cajoled and begged Fallyn to leave with her. She was completely brainwashed. As soon as she could get Fallyn alone she would smack her upside the head and drag her ass out of here if she had to.

Azy squeezed the shard tight against her chest and closed her eyes. Whoever was on the other end of this connection couldn't help her. No one could but Azy herself. But just knowing he was there gave her strength, and she was going to need it.

The Black Witch left Fallyn standing in the cavern alone, her hand still at her throat. Azy would wait a few minutes to see if anyone returned, then she was nabbing Fallyn and getting the hell out of hell.

Fallyn didn't move, like she was in a trance. Azy had seen her do that more than once. She'd also seen her talking to herself, having a one-sided conversation with someone in her head.

The path back down to the cavern floor sloped at a steep enough angle that Azy had to scooch down some of it on her butt. Thank goodness for her scales.

Around the same time as that succubus had given her the golden shard, her scales had developed an extra layer of toughness. She also had a lot more control over her shift than she'd ever had before.

Usually she needed to be around water to bring on any part of the mermaid side of her, but now all she had to do was think about needing more protection and poof, they were there, and not just on her legs either. Pearlescent scales, more white than yellow like her tail, would surface on her arms, neck, and belly too.

The best thing about this new ability was that it shielded her from the unbearable heat. Fallyn had something similar, only her scales were red.

When Azy reached the cavern floor, she glanced around one more time to make sure they were alone and would remain that way. Fallyn hadn't moved and there were no other sounds around. Safe. For now.

"Fallyn, we need to leave. Now." No use plying her with hellos and how are yous.

Fallyn turned and looked genuinely surprised to see Azy. She blinked a few times and tipped her head, hearing a voice that wasn't there. "Shush, Izzy. I can't think with you in my head all the time."

Uh. "It's Azy, not Izzy, remember?"

Fallyn rolled her eyes and swatted at something near her head. There wasn't anything there. Nothing else lived in this forsaken environment, not even creepy crawlies or creepy fly-ies.

"She says I should trust you," Fallyn said, looking at Azy this time.

Okay good. Whoever she was. "She's right. I'm only here to help you."

"Nope. You're not."

This was how pretty much every conversation they'd had went. Azy needed to try something different. She took Fallyn's hand and gave it a tug, leading her across the cavern to one of the tunnels. Surprisingly, Fallyn followed. "Leave with me and I'll show you. There's a better life away from here. We'll get you help."

Fallyn stopped them, dead in their tracks, but didn't release Azy's hand. "From the dragon warriors? I don't think so."

"It doesn't have to be with them. There are humans that can help you too." Like psychiatrists and pharmacists, and reconstructive surgeons.

"Humans are worse than the dragons. They're weak and kill each other for no reason."

She couldn't argue with that. "You're right on both counts. Humans can suck. Some of them aren't so bad though."

Like her father. He'd been one of the good guys. She kept the memories of her father's fight for all that was right and just in the world close to her heart. Sometimes it hurt too much to bring them out, but maybe if she told Fallyn about him and the way love should be, it would break through that wall Kur-Jara and Ereshkigal had built around her mind and heart.

"Fallyn—"

Fallyn gasped and let go of Azy's hand. "Oh no. Azynsa. Run. Hide. He's coming for you."

Azy wasn't sure if the buzzing that started in her chest was her heart skipping several beats or the shard flipping its shit. She grabbed it and vibrated in her hand. The protective scales rippled across her hand.

Fallyn pushed her into the tunnel and she stumbled to the floor. "Don't let him…oh no…them find you. It will mean the end of you. Go. Azynsa," Fallyn's voice broke, "please."

Azy turned to see how close the Black Dragon or his demon dragons were. None were there.

Fallyn ran across the cavern and ducked into one of the side caves. Azy knew from experience that there would be no following her. She knew this maze better than anyone else.

Her heart still beat hard in her chest and the shard in her hand glowed brighter than normal. That burst of adrenaline hadn't helped. It would crash soon enough.

She used the extra light from the shard to make her way through this lesser used part of the caldera. It was cooler here and she retreated to the tunnel the dragons had made when they escaped.

Most of it had collapsed back in on itself, but a few feet up, a crack in the rock was just wide enough for her to squish through, even though she scraped the hell out of her skin the first time she'd tried. She'd called on the scales to shield her after that.

It opened into a cave just wide enough for her to lay down in. Azy pushed rocks and dirt over the crack in the rock so that no one could follow her in or find her hiding spot.

When she was satisfied that she was safe, she collapsed onto the floor. More than exhausted.

One tiny, feathery root with one pale green leaf grew into the space from the ceiling above. Life. Azy clung to it.

There was the lightest touch of magic wrapped around the root, from who or where, Azy didn't know and didn't care. Every once in a while, a drop of dirty, mineral-filled water would cling to the tiny hairs of the plant's root and pooled into the leaf's little cup. It was the only water she'd had access to in weeks.

When she first found the drops, she'd wet her lips and mouth. She was thirsty as... well, hell.

It shouldn't have been enough, but that same magic was in those drops and they sustained her. She lifted her finger to the tip of the leaf and let the droplet fall onto her finger.

The tiniest of reflections glimmered in the little water drop, like the golden mirrors of her mother's people. Azy closed her eyes and knew she was falling asleep but couldn't talk herself into consciousness.

The drop of water in her hand shimmered and grew until she held a hand mirror like the one her mother had intended to leave for her. She'd had this dream before. Many times growing up, but now, it came every time she fell asleep.

In the mirror she didn't see her own reflection but that of a man, a warrior. His hair was a golden blond and his skin was the polar opposite of hers, light to her dark.

She longed to see the contrast of his hands on her body. He was her mate, her soul mate, if the dragons and Fallyn were to be believed. She'd never seen him in dragon form.

Azy was so damn tired she almost wanted to call out to him, ask him to come and rescue her, take care of her.

Even if he was real, she wouldn't do that. She would take care of this herself. She didn't need a protector, a guardian.

Her father had tried to be that for a lot of people. It was what got him killed. If Azy hadn't asked for help that day, he would still be alive.

So, no. She would not ask for anything from this man, whoever he was, except for this connection.

"I'm coming for you, little mermaid," a voice like honey and charm whispered into her mind.

Azy almost dropped the dream mirror. The reflection had never spoken to her before. Could he hear her too? If he could she had to warn him off.

"Don't do that. You'll only get hurt. I'll be fine on my own."

"I don't accept that. I will find you, and when I do I will claim you for my own."

Oh for Jesus sake.

"Don't be a…douchecanoe." She'd never said that word in her life, but it felt like divine intervention had given it to her. Fit perfectly.

The reflection chuckled. "I am coming for you. But I haven't yet gotten what I need to get into the hellhole where you're trapped. Soon though."

"I said don't come down here."

"That isn't an option."

For the first time since her father had died, Azy felt like crying. Oh, god damn it, she was crying. She turned her head away so he wouldn't see.

She didn't cry. She wasn't weak like that.

"Shit. My love. Don't cry. What can I do to help you? It's killing me to be here while you're there."

"I'm not crying. I'm trying not to kill you." She didn't need him to be a dickhead now. This was her respite, her time to recharge.

"You can kill me all you want later. For now, kiss me."

Azy looked back and the mirror was no longer in her hands. The big, muscled chest of a very naked, very sexy man was.

He was here.

He wasn't here.

She could feel his touch. It wasn't real.

"Azynsa, you're fucking beautiful." His fingers caressed her arm, working its way up, skimming so lightly across her skin that it was more like a breeze.

"Uh." She wanted to tell him to stop, but it felt so damn good. Her brain skittered to a total stop and reverse when his fingers skated across her bare breasts.

"When I find you, I'm going to spend a full complete year worshipping your left nipple. Then the next year I'll spend on the right one." He lowered his head and took said left nipple into his mouth.

Azy arched her back, pushing into him. She knew this wasn't real, but she didn't care. She wrapped her hands into his hair and held him to her breast.

He licked and nipped and sent zings of pleasure through her

body. So much so, that she didn't even notice his hand creeping between her legs until it brushed across her curls.

He raised his head and stared into her eyes, his hand hovering over her pussy but not touching. "Let me take care of you Azynsa. Say you want me to."

Well, that blew the mood. It wasn't his fault that his choice of words in asking for her consent was the opposite of what she wanted. Consent was sexy as hell, yes. To be taken care of, no.

"No."

He blinked and then frowned but pulled his hand away. "No?"

"I'll take care of myself, thanks."

He grinned and took her words in the dirtiest of possible ways.

And then he was gone.

Azy jerked awake. The walls of her little cave were trembling and she heard the screech of demon dragons getting close.

She had nowhere to run, nowhere to hide. Maybe it wouldn't be so bad to have someone at her side at times like this.

She huddled into a ball and pushed herself as far into the little space as she could and waited. Either they would find her and kill her, like Fallyn said, or they wouldn't.

Had Fallyn told them where she was? No. She wouldn't, she'd been genuinely concerned that they were coming for Azy.

So how had they found her hiding spot now?

JETTS AND PLANES

*A*nzysa.

He'd seen her, spoken to her, tasted her.

What a beautiful, stubborn ass woman was his mate, and he was a… douchecanoe.

She was his. Of that he was totally sure. The scent of her, the way she arched into his touch. They were going to be mind-blowing in bed.

He'd woken up with a hard-on that regardless of how many times he'd tried to take care of it in the shower this morning, was still pressing against his zipper, straining to get out.

He refused to believe his cock was reacting to Portia's presence, but he wasn't the only walking hard-on at The Lindens today. Portia's allure must be back online after a night of safety and food. She had affected so many of his warriors now that he'd gotten Zon to organize a warrior tournament. Gris hated the idea, but he wasn't as swayed by the allure as the rest of them. Winner got the chance to woo and feed the lovely Portia.

If and when she delivered Jett.

So far, she wasn't having any luck.

Cage sat in the comfy chair next the sun lamp where he liked to hang out and read mystery novels. It was the only light on in the office and it still made Portia squint.

She paced back and forth behind his desk, yelling at the phone. Cajoling and pleading hadn't done a thing so far to convince Jett to even come to The Lindens, much less help Cage get to hell.

Little fucker.

Portia even turned her allure on Jett to no avail. Although that last bit had several dragon warriors who were supposed to be guards knocking down the door. Gris was practically beating them all back with a stick.

Even her tears didn't convince that bastard to come. What, like he had more important things to do, like chasing terrified women through the woods or something?

She had him on speakerphone now and the little shit was being exactly that. A shit.

What he didn't know was that Cage was no Luddite. He used his money to invest in all kinds of tech companies. Including the kind that created and used clandestine ops and all the fun gadgets that went with it. He was tracing this call and a team of his warriors were already en route to capture the bastard. SEAL Team Six had nothing on his guys.

Then again, the SEALs didn't have to fight demon dragons on a daily basis and couldn't use the power of sunshine and wind, and they didn't have wings, or tails, or sharp spiky teeth.

His guys were ready to nab him. Portia keeping Jett on the line now was gravy.

"Any favors I owed you were repaid when I convinced Geshtianna not to send her asshole brother after you. You're persona non-grata in the demon community, I'm the only reason you're not dead."

Portia's face dropped even further at those words. Her body language went from irritated to defeated, despondent.

Nice boyfriend she had there.

Cage had more than enough reasons to push Portia to the edge, but he wasn't a total dick. Enough was enough. He hadn't yet said a word and had instructed her not to mention he was listening.

If Jett had been willing to help because Portia asked, Cage would have been fine with that, but really all he'd needed from her was the connection.

His tablet pinged with a message—perfect timing. He stood and crossed over to her, giving her a little chuck on the chin and a wink. "I'll take it from here, pumpkin."

She scowled at the pet name and stuck out her tongue at him. But, there was relief in her eyes too. Whoever's mate she was had their work cut out for them. Poor lucky bastard.

He tapped a few keys on his tablet, got the response he was looking for, and waited a few moments for the sounds of his team taking Jett down.

Portia glanced at him, a flash of concern in her eyes, when they heard a scuffle, the distinctive sound of dragon fire, and then the line went dead.

A new call came through on his cell phone. He answered on speaker, so she could hear that her precious ex wasn't harmed.

"We have him, sir. ETA one hour," the team leader said.

"Good work. Try not to kill him in the next sixty minutes."

"Will do."

Cage hung up just before Portia poked him in the chest.

"What did you need me for if you already knew where he was? He can't be that far away if they're bringing him back in within an hour."

He pushed her hand away. "He's a slippery little bastard. You were the perfect distraction."

If looks could kill, Portia would be on trial for murdering a Wyvern. "I'm god damn tired of being used."

"Then think of it as payback."

She bit back her retort. Unusual for her. "Are you going to kill him?"

Concern? Was she thinking about how she could help Jett escape? The asshole had done quite a number on her. She seemed both angry and loyal to him at the same time. "Someday. First I need him to answer a few questions."

"Can I be there?"

Would her allure work on Jett? That could be useful. "If you want to help me question him."

"No. I mean when you kill him."

She was bloodthirsty. At least that meant she wasn't going to try to help him escape.

It was hard not to feel protective of Portia. Yes, she'd wronged him, but he fully understood she'd done it out of what she thought was love.

Not like he knew anything about that emotion. He did understand the deep-seated need for connection. He'd sought it with her. Only to be used, but still. He played a part in her story and she in his.

"I need him to get me into hell and back first."

Portia raised an eyebrow. "I can't believe you're going to trust him."

"I'm not. But, I don't have another choice. He'll get me down to Azynsa or every gold dragon from here to eternity will hunt him down."

"It's your ass."

There were a lot more asses on the line that just his. "You've fulfilled your debt to me. You can leave if you want."

"What? You said I could stay if I got Jett for you."

"You can. My warriors are prepared to protect and provide for you as long as you need. They're out on the training field battling for your favor as we speak."

Portia glanced toward the covered window and frowned. "Don't they all hate me for what I did to you?"

"Some do. It's not in the gold dragon nature to hold a grudge. Besides, I believe the power of your allure is back. I still don't feel it, but Gris and Zon have been beating the others back all morning. Which is why I asked them to organize the tournament."

Portia pulled the letter opener from the back of her pants and set the tip, which had been sharpened, directly over his heart. "So, you're just giving me to the winner?"

The door to the office swung open and Gris stared long and hard at Portia's defensive stance before saying anything. The man had a sixth sense when it came to this woman. "Sir?"

"Good timing." Cage used the distraction to disarm Portia. "The team has the rogue and are on their way back in. Please escort our guest to wherever she chooses to go and inform the warriors the tournament is off. She does not wish to...utilize their services."

Gris nodded but not at Cage. Was that relief on his face? Couldn't blame him. Babysitting wasn't exactly in his job description.

Portia looked between the two of them. "I didn't say that. They can fight for me or whatever."

Gris growled quiet and low. "It's your choice, succubus."

Maybe Gris wasn't the right dragon to watch over Portia in Cage's absence. He had some serious hate going on for her. Zon might be better for this particular chore.

One more thing to add to his to-do list for the next few hours as he prepared to go to Africa. If he was going to trust Gris to take over the Wyr, it was now or never.

"I've got a lot to do before I leave tonight. You two work it out. I've got my guide and one way or another, will be in hell by tonight."

Gris glared at Portia to hide his concern, unsuccessfully, but he tried. "Yes, sir."

The two of them left, biting at each other with words and growls and glares. They were either going to kill each other or end up in bed together.

Within the hour, his team had Jett wrestled into the red dragon's guest suite and chained to the wall. Yes, the red dragons were kinky bastards. That particular attribute was about to come in handy.

Cage cleared the room when he entered, under protest from the team. But, Jett wasn't going anywhere. Those chains had been forged by the First Dragon himself. No one – man – or dragon, could escape them.

He propped himself against the edge of the bed, crossing his legs as if this was a conversation about the weather, not his mate and every gold mate's life out there.

"What will it take, rogue?"

Jett didn't struggle against the chains. He did watch and wait. "I wondered when you'd quit hiding behind Portia's skirts. As nice as the view of her plump ass is, it's a wonder you came out at all."

Maybe he should have brought Portia in to torture this asshole a bit.

"Yes, something we can agree on. You used her, she used me, now I get to use you."

A puff of smoke drifted up from Jett's nose. "What is it you actually want—gold?"

"For you to name your price. Everyone has one."

"You can't afford what I want."

"Try me."

Jett was silent but not because he didn't want anything. Cage could practically see the cogs turning in his mind.

It was well known that Cage was the wealthiest dragon in the world. When one's family had been collecting fine things and building wealth like greedy bastards for centuries, one had some cash to spare on bribing people to do what they wanted.

He was prepared to give up his entire fortune if it meant he could rescue Azynsa and make it possible for the gold dragons to get their mates.

"There is something I want, but I'm not prepared to reveal the details to you."

Then it wasn't money. When he and Portia had been together, Jett had been after a soul shard. Well, Cage didn't have one of those to give.

"What do you suggest then?"

"I want a future favor. To be named and delivered upon my request."

Whatever it was this black dragon wanted from him would hurt, or he'd simply say what it was now. It was a negotiating tactic Cage understood well. There wasn't a damn thing he could do about it because he would do whatever Jett needed. "As long as it does no harm to my mate, or any dragon's mate for that matter, you may have your favor. I will not fulfill it or let you go until you give me what I want."

"You dragons have me now, but I will not ever give up my freedom. What do you want from me?"

That was the only in that Cage needed.

"Not much. All I need is a guide."

"Where – ah. You're going to hell."

In more ways than one. The rogue may be trouble, but he wasn't stupid.

"You should have said. Anything that will let me make Kur-Jara's life hard, I'm down for. Now you owe me a favor and I intend to cash it in, dragon."

Fuck a lucky duck.

"I will honor my debt, but only upon Azynsa's safe return to The Lindens."

With or without him. Cage would make arrangements with Gris to get Jett whatever he asked for in case he didn't make it back himself.

"Out of the caldera. I'm not hiring on to be her nursemaid

once she's out. I've got other business to take care of."

"Fine." He wasn't discussing semantics. "We will transport you to Africa tonight."

That gave him enough time to get Gris up to speed on all of the plans, including what to do in case he didn't make it, and fly down to Western Africa. Not on his own wings, but he had a backup.

"I don't need your commandos to take me anywhere. I'll honor my word. This arrangement benefits me as much as you. Find me tonight at Candy's, not far from the Malabo airport."

"Who's Candy? Your new stripper girlfriend?"

"It's an Irish pub." Cage could practically hear the fuck-off in Jett's reply.

The fates, or the White Witch, had known what they were doing, he had to trust in that. Because what else did he have now that his dragon was lost?

"Tonight then." Cage didn't wait for Jett to agree. He had a few short hours to make final preparations in case of his death and do everything he could think of to mentally and physically prepare for the upcoming battle.

Gris and Zon could take care of getting Jett released and put a tail on him to Malabo.

Cage took care of his Wyvern business and left for the airfield before dusk. On his way, he felt a pull toward one of his lairs. Cage rarely visited this one even though it was the closest, partly because he preferred to have most of his treasure right out in the open.

The Lindens was filled with antiquities and high-end modern design. He also had some stashed in a monastery high in the mountains of Nepal, where the air was so thin that it felt like he was in the sky. But, like any smart wyvern he had his hoard divided into several locations just in case any of them were compromised. That didn't happen very often, but Jacob's lair under his villa in the Czech Republic had been discovered by demon dragons not that long ago.

Cage drove into the Danish countryside until he reached a hilly area. He hated being underground, so the cave hidden in the brush at the top of the hill was a good compromise. He'd spent years here as a child, secreting away his favorite treasures and carving out the rock to let slivers of sunshine into the cave. This had been his secret hideout, the place he went to practice shifting into his dragon form as a youngling. There was an old magic in these hills that had drawn him to it and helped him master his shifting skills.

It was almost uncomfortable to come here now knowing that he had lost the majority of that hard work, but something had led him here and his gut told him to listen. Perhaps there was armor or a weapon hidden in this lair that might be able to help him survive on this quest.

He hiked up into the hills for a good hour, feeling the wards that had been placed to deter both humans and other paranormal beings alike from finding his cave.

To him they were nothing more than little zips of electricity, but to anyone snooping they would get a sense of dread or fear from being here. The closer he got, the more the magic swelled. Oh yeah, whatever was pulling him really wanted to make sure he didn't leave without finding it.

Cage stepped through a layer of creeping vines that covered the cave entrance and into the darkness. He called upon the light of the sun and a glowing orb formed in his hand and lit his way. He walked past suits of armor, chests filled with gold, and ancient weapons that wouldn't do him any good if he came face-to-face with the Black Dragon, like swords. It didn't take him long to find what had been calling to him. Tucked back onto a natural shelf along the cave wall a golden hand mirror glowed in the darkness.

He vaguely remembered being attracted to the object. It was

very old, and the handle was decorated in jewels and carvings of scales that rippled as he touched it. He'd always imagined it had been a present from a dragon to his mate.

Great.

What was he supposed to do with a mirror?

For a fraction of a second, he thought he saw a face in the reflection that was not his own. It was gone before he could blink.

Okay, fine. Maybe the universe was looking out for him by making sure he had a gift for Azynsa.

Cage wrapped the mirror in a scrap from an old tapestry and pocketed it. It felt warm against his thigh.

He returned to his car and raced to the small private airfield, wanting to get in the air as soon as possible.

This was no average airport. The hangers were filled with vintage airplanes, mostly from World War II. The shack that served as the radio tower was filled with vintage flyers too. Mostly veterans of the past few wars.

Cage liked to flaunt his money, but he also used it for good causes. The majority of the men who hung around here had been severely injured in the line of duty and were forced to give up flying for their countries.

Cage started a little organization to allow these vets to fly. He understood their need to be in the air more now than ever before.

His father had balked when he'd first wanted gold dragons to learn to fly airplanes when they began to appear at the beginning of the twentieth century.

He'd realized humans were in the air to stay and defied his father by joining up with the RAF during the second world war. His compatriots had treated him like a young whipper-snapper, or so they'd called him. To them he was only about eighteen back then, even though at the start of the war he'd been exactly one-hundred years old.

They'd given him his due when they saw how naturally he commanded his plane through the air. He'd taken to airplanes like a duck in water, err, the sky.

Since then, a handful of other gold dragons of his generation had become pilots in every military with aviators in the world. The ones who'd served their time rotated through on assignment to staff this place and make sure the planes and the pilots got in and out of the air safely.

Cage had a lot of other charities he supported, but this was the one he liked hanging out at the most.

He called ahead and had one of his more modern little turbo-props fueled and ready for the flight to Malabo. There was only time for a super quick check-in with his dragons, who confirmed he was set and ready to go. His plane was the only one cleared for takeoff.

There were lots of vets hanging around today and he hated to ground them but, just today, his flight needed to take priority.

One of his vets stood next to his plane, examining the props. He still had the build of a warrior, despite the prosthetic arm. Cage could tell this man had stories he'd like to hear. If he made it back, this guy would be the first one he'd seek out to go flying with. Today, he'd have to ask him to return to the hangar.

"Excuse me, sir."

Sparkling eyes that had so many facets in them Cage couldn't tell what color they were stared across at him. "I wondered when you'd finally show up. Taking your sweet time getting in the air."

"Yeah, I had to stop—" How did this strange old guy know anything about Cage's itinerary?

"Son, let me tell you a thing or two about independent women."

First, he'd chided Cage about taking his time, and now he wanted to chat about women? Just who was this? No ordinary aging veteran, that was for sure.

"As you stated, sir, I need to get in the air ASAP."

"You can bluster and blow, plead, and persuade them all you want, but once they've made up their mind about something, well you just better go with it, because there's no changing it. Remember that, will you?"

A banked power unlike anything Cage had experienced rolled out with every word the man said. He had no idea who this old-timer was, but there was no mistake about the feeling of awe and deference.

"Okay. I'll keep that in mind."

"Take my sugar lips, for instance. She hates it when I call her that, but damn her kisses are so sweet." The man chuckled and slapped Cage on the shoulder. "She's got a mind that she can do something about the troubles in this world. I thought we'd given that all up years ago. But here I am smack dab in the middle of her matchmaking schemes."

Matchmaking?

"Now, don't get me wrong, I'd like to see you boys all find your mates. It's a damn shame your fathers couldn't figure out how to combat that spell. Had we known that bitch was going to get involved, we might not have left."

A shiver rolled down the back of Cage's neck and all the hairs on his body stood on end.

"We had to protect our girl. You understand that, don't you?" The man looked at Cage and must have seen the shock in his eyes. Or maybe it was the fact that his jaw was hanging open wide enough for a fly, or a dragon, or a dragonfly to swoop in. "No, I can see that you don't. You will though when your own show up."

His own? Really important information was being discussed in this conversation, but damn if Cage had an idea what any of it meant.

A woman, who looked to be about the same age as the cryptic veteran crossed the tarmac and wrapped her arms around him. She wore flowing white pants with a crisp pleat down the front, an aviator's jacket that was usually brown with white wool, but hers was pure as snow, and a long, flowing, silk aviator's scarf.

"Did you give him the sword?"

"I was just getting to that, sugar lips. We had some mate stuff to discuss first."

"Oh God. Did he give you the dozen orgasms speech?"

Cage's vision wavered. The two figures before him shimmered like mirages. He thought he shook his head, but he really wasn't sure.

"Hey, that's good advice for any young dragon about to become a mate. You certainly liked it when we first mated."

She leaned in and whispered something in the man's ear that had his eyes going wide.

"Okay, son. Gotta go. Places to go, people to see, orgasms to be given." He shoved a shining golden sword into Cage's hands. "Here's your blade. Don't be giving it to any Annunaki, even if they ask for it."

The woman took her scarf off and wrapped it around his neck. "We can't come down and help this time. The Galla demons won't be fooled again, but Ninshubar will be waiting when you get out."

The couple faded right before his eyes and when he blinked, they were gone.

"Oh, did you tell him about…"

"Damn, forgot. Be right back."

The man popped up in front of Cage again. "Listen, when you've got your head between her legs try—"

"No, not that," a disembodied voice chastised.

"Hmm. What? Oh, right. The power is when the two become one." He disappeared again.

Cage was left standing next to his plane holding a sword. What the hell was he supposed to do with a sword and a mirror?

MIRROR, MIRROR

She was covered in dust and dirt, and it would take forever to dig herself back out of her little hidey hole. But, Azy was alive, and so was the little root. More of it was exposed and the droplets of water were bigger now too.

The demon dragons had screeched and clawed and rumbled through the tunnel next to her but hadn't found her. She wasn't entirely sure they'd been after her. They were freaking out about something though.

Most demon dragons she'd encountered were dumber than the rocks they lived under, and only a few could even speak. She'd heard a few of them say the word "gold" over and over.

At their cores they were dragons, so maybe they were excited about a cache of gold they'd found or something. Azy had found all kinds of treasures hidden in caves, half abandoned tunnels, and alcoves. It was pretty much all worthless to her, except for the bits of leather armor she'd found. Gold coins and jeweled trinkets didn't do much good when you're fighting against demons.

She dug herself out a peek hole and made sure there were no prying eyes around before she crawled out into the tunnel. She'd hidden much longer than usual, and she was freaking starving. She had no idea what demon dragons ate, but it smelled an awful lot like rotting flesh. Fallyn had real food and if and when Azy ever dragged her out of here, she would be immediately teaching her about the wonders of late-night drive-through.

In the past few years living with the Mami Wata, eating fish and other sea life she had to catch herself, she had often wished for Long John Silvers. Ooh, or the church's Friday fish fry during Lent. She'd had enough raw fish to last a lifetime, she wouldn't be searching out the sushi place anytime soon.

Azy crept along the tunnel, headed for one of the small caves Fallyn spent most of her time in. She might not have any desire to leave, but the woman truly did not belong down here. On more than one occasion she had sent or shared her food with Azy. She never appeared in anything but human form, but she wasn't entirely human. She did have a strong sense of what was right and wrong, and that included empathy, unlike any of the other creatures down here. Azy didn't have any idea where she could have learned to have concern for anyone beside herself. It certainly wasn't from the Black Dragon or Ereshkigal, the witch.

Fallyn wasn't in the first cave Azy searched, nor in the second. There was one more place she could try but really didn't want to. There was the tunnel she saw Fallyn go in and out of a lot, but so did the Black Dragon.

She had to try. If she didn't, the rumble from her stomach would be loud enough to draw demon dragons from miles away. Thus, door number three it was.

Normally, Azy had to carefully pick her way through the tunnels waiting for groups of demon dragons to move away before she could continue. Today, the caves and tunnels were empty. Eerily empty. Where in the hell – ha ha – was everyone?

She crept up the forbidden tunnel and heard a thwack thwack thwack up ahead. A faint light shined into the dark. The thwacking repeated, always in threes. Azy practically tiptoed, trying her best not to be heard. Except, she stumbled on some loose pebbles and skidded on her hands and knees, causing more rocks to tumble around her.

"Shitting shit bricks," she whispered and stilled, waiting to see if the thwacker had heard and was coming out to thwack her.

"What are you doing here, Azynsa?" Fallyn's voice floated from out of the cave.

"How did you know it was me?"

"Because it was you."

Right. Azy got up, pulled the pebbles out of her hands and brushed off her leather pants. She glanced into the cave and just stared. No wonder none of the other random treasure hoards she'd stumbled across had any weapons. They were all here. This wasn't a cave. It was an armory. Not one filled with guns and bombs but with lots and lots of sharp pointy things.

She imagined a thousand years of knights in shining armor trying to rescue the fair princess, for the Black Dragon to have this many swords, scythes, and – seriously? Yep, that was a pile of maces.

In the middle of all of these ancient weapons, Fallyn stood with a bucket of daggers next to her. She didn't even glance back at Azy, simply picked up three daggers and threw them in rapid succession toward her target. A form that looked remarkably like the upper torso of a dragon. A red dragon.

The daggers flew through the air, sticking into the target with extreme precision. One in the heart and two in the eyeballs. *Thwack thwack thwack.*

Jesus.

"You shouldn't be here. Don't touch any of my things."

"By things do you mean all of these knives and swords?"

"Yes, they're mine."

Azy raised her hands to show she wasn't touching anything. "Why do you have all of this?"

Fallyn stopped throwing her daggers for a moment. She

glanced at Azy and tilted her head a few degrees to the right. "Do your people not hoard things?"

Oh. That's what this was. Fallyn had been raised by a dragon, so it made sense that she would learn his ways. "I suppose we do. The Mami Wata like their fair share of shiny things."

"But not you?"

"Not really. What I like to hoard doesn't do well underwater." Books had always been her solace. It was strange to think she hadn't read in years. She wondered if there was a chance that Fallyn had any. The woman definitely liked her bling and some old romance novels had those gold raised letters on them. Everywhere she looked, she only saw shiny, spiky metal. Except in one corner.

"Are those… Christmas ornaments?"

Fallyn dropped the dagger she had been about to throw into the bucket and moved swiftly in front of the display. "I don't know what Christmas is. Don't touch these."

She tried to block Azy's view with her body. There was no way she could. Ornaments hung from the tips of hundreds of blades that had been reshaped to form a macabre sort of Christmas tree, or bush, or crown of thorns. Some looked like they were a hundred years old. Many though, were practically brand-new. She was sure because, directly over Fallyn's shoulder, was a Pokémon ornament.

"Where did you get all of these?"

Fallyn glared at her but must have decided she wasn't trying to steal anything. "I collect them."

Azy had never seen Fallyn leave hell, although she had only been down here a few weeks and it was June. Maybe Fallyn only went outside for Christmas shopping and plundering ancient castles while she was at it.

She wanted to ask more because while she was determined to get Fallyn out of hell, she didn't actually have any idea of the route out of here. She had been dragged in through an underground tunnel that opened to a water cave. In all her secretive explorations she had yet to find that way out.

The dragons had dug their way out, but she knew at least one of them controlled the earth element. If she could get Fallyn to open up about the Christmas ornaments, maybe she could get her to reveal how to get to the surface.

"How –" Azy stopped midsentence because Fallyn's face had gone white, or actually yellow. The shard hanging from Azy's neck decided to turn on like an old-fashioned lightbulb. Its glow filled the room. She grabbed it to try to dampen its light, but the rays shined through her fingers like she was trying to block the sun.

"No, no, no, no, no." Fallyn shook her head and wrapped her arms around herself. "Mate, mate, mate, mate."

"What's happening, Fallyn?"

Fallyn grabbed up a sword and pointed it directly at Azy's chest. "He's coming. It's the end of you. Choose now. Are you with him or with me?"

"Him who? The Black Dragon? Then I'm with you." This might finally be it. Something about the light of the shard had put the fear of God into Fallyn. This was the opportunity Azy had been waiting for. "Let's run, run far away, where he can never hurt you again."

"Not red. Gold." Fallyn turned and shoved her way through the ornaments, looking for something. She snatched a particularly shiny one from a blade tip and shoved it at Azy. "Gold."

The ornament was a polished piece of glass etched with the words - Baby's First Christmas 1976. It wasn't the words that she saw—it was the face.

The face of her mate.

He was somewhere here in hell. And not only surrounded by demon dragons, but that son of the black dragon was attacking too.

He had a golden sword raised and black dragon next to him

bared its fangs. It lunged at her mate and Azy screamed out. "No, oh God, no.

She'd never met this man, and certainly didn't want to have any feelings for him, but the fates had decided otherwise for her. She knew deep in her heart that if he were killed now, right before her eyes, she would not recover from the grief. It would be worse even than when her father had died.

The Black Dragon snapped at her mate's neck but did not draw blood. It snagged a white scarf from around his neck. The dragon must have communicated telepathically because her mate, who looked just as shocked as Azy felt, took the scarf and held it out, moving through the crowd of dragons.

They didn't attack. Why didn't they attack? "Why aren't they moving, is it a trap?"

Azy didn't know how she push those words out, because there was no air in her lungs. It had all been sucked out and she couldn't seem to get herself to inhale.

"Annunaki. They mustn't let them pass." Fallyn watched just as rapt as Azy.

In another moment they saw two Annunaki standing like sphinxes guarding the path through the desert. Her mate handed the scarf to one of them. Its face remained emotionless, but it stepped to the side and outstretched its arm to indicate that they could continue.

"Holy fuck, Jett. What the hell was that all about?" His words floated through the mirror, muffled like they were watching bad TV.

With the sound of her mate's voice, Azy found the ability to breathe again.

The black dragon shifted back into its human form and patted her mate on the back. "The first gate of hell, Cage. Hope you brought some more trinkets to give to them, because we have six more to go."

"The seven gates of hell? You couldn't have warned me?"

"Nope."

They watched the two men go through five more of the passageways guarded by the Annunaki. At each, Cage - such a strange name - removed another piece of clothing and handed it over, until he was bare footed and bare chested. All he had left for the last gate was his sword and his pants.

She wouldn't mind seeing his butt, however, she'd been naked in hell. It wasn't fun. When they reached the Annunaki, Jett indicated that Cage should hand over the sword.

"Can't do it. Someone told me not to give it up. So, pants it is."

The Annunaki went from its usual stoic face and stance to a monster in a moment.

"I don't think it wants your undies." That was the last thing Azy heard before Jett shifted back into his dragon again and Cage raised his sword. Why didn't he shift too?

A river of demon dragons ascended on them. Cage slashed and chopped as fast as he could, turning the enemy to instant black stains. He wouldn't be able to hold out long in his human form.

"Oh no. Why are they attacking now?"

Azy turned, but Fallyn was no longer watching along with her. She was at her bucket o'death, shoving daggers into pockets, up her sleeve, and one down her shirt.

"The seventh gate is death. One cannot pass into the underworld if they are alive."

Shit. "I don't understand. We're not dead."

"You didn't pass through the gates to get here." Damn it, hell was a confusing ass place, and nobody seemed to know all the rules.

Cage yelled, his voice coming through loud and clear through the mirror now. "What do you mean you can't kill an Annunaki? And where the fuck am I supposed to go, you bastard?"

Azy grabbed up one of the swords and dropped it like it's hot. Because it was. She reached for another, and it fell over. She tried one more time, finding a sword with a dragon inlaid into the handle. It fit into her hand perfectly. Not that she knew how to use it. It couldn't be that hard to at least maim a few demon dragons. "Where is this? I have to go to him."

Fallyn shook her head. "Why would you choose someone who will end you?"

"I'm not choosing him, I'm saving his ass. I don't have time for this. He's not going to hurt me, he's my mate."

"Mates are evil, but you are not. But you are a mate, but you are not." Fallyn frowned and shoved more daggers into her pockets.

"I don't have time for your riddles. Where are they?"

"At the seventh gate."

Argh. "How do I get there?"

"Run."

"Fallyn, I'm going to break every single one of your Christmas ornaments into teeny tiny pieces unless you tell me exactly how to find Cage, right now."

Fallyn didn't like that one bit. She was in Azy's face in an instant. Literal fire burned in her eyes and she smelled of smoke and brimstone.

Azy didn't back down, not an inch. She'd learned real young not to.

Even when Fallyn withdrew one of her daggers, Azy didn't flinch. "How do I find Cage?"

Fallyn glared, the fires inside of her burning hard. Then she lifted the dagger and tapped the shard around Azy's neck with the tip, making the crystal ting. "It will lead you to him."

At first Azy thought it was another of the damn cryptic messages, but then she remembered how the shard glowed earlier. That had to have been when Cage had first entered the caldera.

Yes. She bolted for the entryway to this cave of wonders, grabbing the mirrored ornament on her way.

"Hey, don't touch my stuff."

Azy ran, and she ran, and she ran. The shard got brighter, until she'd take a wrong turn and the shard went dark. Damn it. At this rate Cage would be dead by the time she found him.

The only luck she was having was that the Black Dragon, the Black Witch, and the demon dragons all seemed to be nowhere around.

Her lungs and muscles were burning. She was not used to using her legs this way anymore. A slow jog was all she was managing at the moment. The shard was glowing again, so at least she was going in the right direction.

She held the ornament up, trying to see what was going on. It was dark. Her heart, which had just been pounding hard, skipped a beat. Did that mean Cage was dead?

"Cage, where are you?" she whispered at the mirror.

"Azynsa?" That was his voice. He was alive.

The view in the mirror fumbled around and then she was looking at his face again. His skin was marred by a giant burn mark that started at his hairline and went all the way down his face, slicing through his eyebrow and cheek.

She recognized that kind of wound. Fire whip.

"Can you hear me? How does this thing work?" The view tilted and it looked like he was banging on the side of the ornament.

He must have a mirror on his end too. "Cage. Where are you?"

"We're pinned down behind an outcropping of rocks, but that's all I can tell you."

"I'm coming. I'm getting close." The glow from the shard was brighter than ever before.

Azy also thought she heard the screeches of demon dragons and the clang of a metal sword on rocks up ahead. Yes, she did.

"This is not the way I imagined first hearing those words from your mouth."

Seriously? He was bringing up sex now?

She grinned despite herself. No, no. There would be no liking this man just because he could keep a sense of humor in a rough situation. She would not let his good looks go to her head. She needed her head if she was going to make it through the rest of this day alive.

"Keep it in your pants there, buddy. I wouldn't want you to lose any important bits before we get a chance to use them."

That was not what she meant to say. Not out loud.

Stupid head. Hadn't she just decided there would be no flirting? Besides, only a crazy person would get their flirt on in the middle of a battle with demon dragons. She needed to stay sane here.

"Oh, I plan to use it, not lose it." Cage said that at the same time as swinging his sword and running through a demon dragon who had dropped into his hiding place.

Jesus, that was close.

Azy saw where the tunnel she'd been following opened up. It was a steep climb to that cavern. Some pseudo-stairs had been carved into the incline. There was barely enough room for her toes to get a grip as she climbed. There were fresh scratch marks all along the floor, and it seemed that this was the same path the demon dragons had used.

This was a new area to her. She thought she had explored almost all of the bottom level of the caldera, but the route the shard had taken her on she never would have found on her own.

Her instincts told her they were much closer to the surface than the level she normally spent her time on.

At the top of the steep staircase, she peeked over the ledge and into the ensuing battle. Two Annunaki demons had their great feathered wings out and were divebombing a black dragon, tearing at his scales with their beaks, beating it with their fists, like some kind of dark demonic angels. Demon dragons were surrounding it. Each time one would try to join in the attack Cage with his golden sword would pop up from behind the rocks and chop off its head, or slice it open, turning dozens of them to ash.

Azy recognized the black dragon. He had brought her food and water when she had first been kidnapped. She had thought he was just a more intelligent or more developed demon. She'd never gotten a good look at him like this before and hadn't realize that he was significantly more than those pawns.

"They've got to be coming from somewhere. Find it, get out. I can't hold them back much longer."

Cage's head popped up again and quickly surveyed the small cavern. The place had many dark alcoves where demon dragons were manifesting. No wonder she hadn't seen any in the tunnels, they were all here, or on their way here. That had to mean Kur-Jara wasn't far behind.

"The bastards are coming from everywhere."

"I know there is a side tunnel in here somewhere. Fucking find it."

That was Azy's cue. She climbed out of the tunnel and raised the sword over her head, She-Ra Princess of Power style. Her shard lit up the room as if the sun was suddenly shining underground, and a warmth and power seeped into her, giving her strength. Demon dragons shrank back and whined at the power of the light.

Okay, now what?

Cage had sunk to one knee, and both he and the black dragon looked over at her. In fact, every eye in the room was on her. Out of the side of her mouth she stage-whispered to the two of them, "Come on."

One of the demon dragons shook off the effects of the bright light and screeched out at her. "Mate. Get mate. AllFather want."

The room erupted into answering screeches, and en masse they moved toward her.

"Shit." She extended the sword out in front of her because that was going to do anything. "Bring it on, motherfuckers."

The black dragon jumped in front of her and spread his wings wide, blowing a swath of fire, eviscerating the front row of demons. "Go, go, go."

Cage barreled out from behind the outcropping of rocks and crashed into Azy, taking them both tumbling down the steps and into the tunnel.

They landed with an oomph at the bottom, him on top of her, but she was cradled in his arms so she'd barely felt a thing. He'd taken the brunt of the fall but didn't seem hurt by it.

He rolled so he wasn't crushing her, and she ended up straddling him.

"That's more like it. Hello, mate. Nice to meet you."

CLAIMED

*F*irst Dragon, above and below, Azynsa straddling him was the most beautiful sight under the sun. She was finally in his arms and her dark skin and long black hair was calling for him to touch and tease.

Before another second passed he needed to mark her, claim her, unite their souls for all time. He knew that just as he'd known a new power had sunk into him when he'd seen her. Both had hit him so damn hard, it had knocked him to his knees.

He couldn't feel any stronger, except if he had his dragon back. That part of him still felt empty, but the warmth of having his mate by his side filled that hole with the strength of a thousand suns.

"*Get up, you damn fools, and run.*" Jett whooshed over their heads and farther down the tunnel. Not far behind him was the horde of demon dragons.

He thought there had been a lot of them at the battle he'd fought with Jakob and Ciara. This amounted to ten times that. They screeched and came at them like pissed off ants whose hill had been smashed.

Who cared how many there were or how angry they were.

Cage had found his mate and now they were going to fight their way out of here.

He and Azynsa scrambled to their feet and he grabbed her hand. He shouted to Jett's behind. "Lead the way, oh black–souled one."

Together, they ran, twisting and turning through a maze of tunnels. Demon dragons popped up at every corner. Jett dispatched the first few with his talons or his fire, until they figured out where the weakness was. Mainly Cage and Azynsa.

"To where? Now that they have seen you and your mate, they will be everywhere. Kur-Jara won't be far behind. He wants her bad. The demon dragons are all wound up about it."

One of the little bastards popped up behind them. Azynsa squealed and shoved her blade right through its eye.

That was fucking sexy as hell. He'd known she was a badass, but to see it in person was hot. He'd love to spar with her some-day, just as foreplay. First, they had to escape.

"Can we get out the same way Jakob and Ky did?" Jett was turning out to be a shitty guide.

"Not unless you are a green dragon and not a gold one, or your mate there has some special powers I don't know about."

They hit a dead end and both he and Jett turned to look at Azynsa.

"What do you want from me? I can turn into half a fish. Unless you think these guys want a dragon fish sandwich for dinner, that's not going to help." What she didn't say, but that was clear in her voice, was that she thought the two of them were dumbasses.

God, he could kiss her right here and now. Smart mouth with a sense of humor in a damn tight situation. Adorable. However, he would save kissing for later when they weren't all about to die.

A great roar reverberated through the tunnel followed by a swath of fire that disintegrated the majority of the demon drag-ons. The remaining ones shrank back.

Unless that was miraculously Match, they were about to get a visit from the Black Dragon himself.

The only way out was to fight. There was no way he was making it through six out of the seven gates of hell, surviving an attack by Annunaki and demon dragons, and actually finding Azynsa alive and in good shape, to die at the hands of that son of a bitch. He was still weak, and a mirror and a sword weren't helping him come up with anyway out of this situation.

Cage was no God damned knight in shining armor here to slay the dragon.

Azynsa gripped his hand tighter. "Anyone got any bright ideas on what to do now?"

Oh, fuck yeah. Bright was exactly the right idea. He yanked the mirror off his belt and shoved it into her hand. "Hold this."

He traded the mirror for her sword, shoving the extra blade into his belt. He may need it later.

Not at all how he had planned to gift the mirror to her, but maybe he would not die in the next twenty-seven seconds and could do a better job later. Azynsa stared at the gold and glass and gasped.

"Where did you get my mother's mirror?"

"Later. Hold it up and out like a cross at an exorcism."

"Whatever you're planning, hurry the fuck up." Jett lifted his snout and blew his own fire back into the tunnel. *"Because that is only going to hold him off for about three and half seconds."*

"When I say go, point that mirror right at the Black Dragon's eyes. Jett, when she does, hit him with everything you've got and then grab us. We'll have only an instant to get by him and back on the run."

Neither of them had time to agree to his plan because just then, the Black Dragon showed up.

Its huge body filled the only exit, and it sauntered in like it owned the place, which it did.

Cage held his sword out with one hand, keeping the demon

dragons at bay, and cupped his other hand, concentrated every shred of the sunlight inside of him into a dense ball. When he opened his fist, the light filled the area around the dead end in a blinding flash.

"Go, love. Hit him with the light."

The initial explosion of light diminished and Azynsa was right there with the mirror manipulating the reflected beam directly at the Black Dragon's face like a laser.

The Black Dragon growled and recoiled. Azynsa had to adjust and maneuver so that the light continued to hit him. She found exactly the sweet spot and drilled that beam of light directly into his black eyeball. When she did, Jett blasted the Black Dragon with a burst of flames and threw his own body at its chest.

The distraction of sunlight in this bleak underground hell and the fact that Black Dragon must not have expected them to put up much of a fight gave them the advantage, because, even though Jett's body was half the size of the King of Hell, they tumbled backward into the wall. The cave all around them shook and rocks tumbled from the ceiling.

Jett thrashed and pounded at his opponent, not following through with grabbing the two of them and flying out of there.

Azynsa could no longer focus the mirror with Jett and the Black Dragon fighting each other. Cage pulled the power of the sun back inside himself.

Good, he'd have some energy for later.

He slashed at the demon dragons nearest them who disappeared, not into the black puffs of ash and smoke with their death but teleported across the room.

Each time he struck one of them, the sword hit flesh and bone but then glided through it like a puff of wind. They reappeared around the Black Dragon.

Great. Another new trick to fight against. At least they weren't able to get to Azynsa and her mirror.

Jett hit the Black Dragon again with his tail, but it ducked, and the spikes on Jett's tail hit the wall, causing more of a cave in. Jett did not relent, which was not the plan. Cage could see there would be no reaching the rogue in his current state of mind. If ever there was a berserker dragon, Jett was it.

He was out for the Black Dragon's blood. Cage should have guessed this was Jett's original intent.

The Black Dragon retaliated with a swipe of its own tail, which caught Jett in the shoulder. He cracked against the wall and a fissure snaked its way up the rock. Cage glimpsed the tiniest bit of light leaking through that crack. Whatever was on the other side of that wall was the only escape route.

The ground shook like an earthquake under the force of the dragons' battle. It wouldn't be long now.

Cage pressed his mouth to Azynsa ear, which might have been necessary for her to hear him over the din, but it was certainly no hardship. The scent of rain over the ocean enveloped him and he would never forget it. Damn it, he needed to concentrate on getting her to safety not on how he couldn't wait to taste her. "On his next hit, run."

"Where?"

Jett didn't miss a beat and rolled with the next hit, using the Black Dragon's momentum to yank it up and into the air. It struck the wall hard enough to not only expand the crack like Cage had thought it would, but broke right through and into a huge cavern lit by pools of lava.

"There - go, go, go." He pushed Azynsa forward, and she was off and running without his help.

Azynsa continued to hold the mirror in front of her, which he couldn't blame her for, seeing as she had no other weapon anymore. Cage slashed at more demon dragons, who this time appeared in the open cavern as he struck them. Slick bastards.

Jett flew at the Black Dragon, who was still pulling himself up from the floor of the larger cavern it had fallen into. The Black Dragon twisted at the last moment and tossed Jett over his back, passing him. Jett used his wings to slow himself down, but it was too quick for him to expand them fully and he skidded to the edge of a pool of lava.

"I know where we are now, and I think I can get us to my hiding place." Azynsa pointed to a tunnel not far from them. If Jett continue to battle the Black Dragon, they could probably slip away unnoticed. Cage gritted his teeth. The rogue might be a total dickhead, he didn't deserve this fate.

Damn, Cage needed his dragon now. Together the two of them might be able to injure the Black Dragon at least, and at best capture him. But Cage didn't have his dragon.

"Ready to try that trick again?"

Before she could agree, Jett yelled into their heads, "*Get her the fuck out of here. I will find you for that favor later.*"

There was no time for an argument. If the rogue thought he could take care of himself, Cage had to believe it. His number one priority was Azynsa. Together the two of them would figure out a way out of hell, with or without Jett. The Black Dragon hurdled himself at Jett again, and this was the perfect opportunity to get away. Cage kept them both close to the wall and worked his way over to the tunnel she had indicated. He ducked inside to make sure the coast was clear, expecting her to come in right behind him. She stood frozen at the entryway.

"Azynsa, come on. The coast is clear. Only you know the way."

She didn't move. In fact, she wasn't even breathing. Cage tried to pull her into the tunnel, but she swatted him away.

"He'll be fine. Let's go."

"But, she won't," Azynsa said and pointed to the other side of the cavern.

Cage popped his head back out and saw an old woman appear there, gripping the arm of another younger woman, hauling her along.

"You lied, child," she croaked. "Now, face the consequences."

The old woman shoved the girl between the Black Dragon and Jett. She would be crushed between the two combatants.

"No." Azynsa jumped forward, reaching her arms out as if she could save the woman who was at least ten meters away.

Cage grabbed for Azynsa but missed her and she ran into the fray.

The Black Dragon, who had his claws aimed directly at Jett's chest via the woman, pulled up and swerved at the last moment, catching her in the face and snapping her head back. She crashed into the floor and rolled toward the lava pool.

Azynsa dove and reached the woman before she could tumble into the liquid hot rock. Cage put on a burst of speed and caught up with them both, pulling them back away from the edge.

"Well, what do we have here? A weak warrior, a missing mate, and a traitor. The exact three things I've been looking for." The Black Dragon landed and hulked over the three of them. "Release her."

Cage put himself between the Black Dragon and the women. The fucker would have to go through him first. Although, it would be nice if Jett continued his berserking.

"Your new friend can't help you now." The Black Dragon lowered his wings and stepped to the side. Jett was behind him and pinned to the ceiling with absolutely nothing holding him there.

"The Black Witch has him now," Azynsa whispered from behind him. She had shoved the mirror into her belt like it was a sword and cradled the head of the woman, who was unconscious, in her hands.

This woman was obviously important to the Black Dragon. Maybe he could trade her for Jett. What if she was another mate, kidnapped by him? That was a no-win situation. If Cage had learned anything in his two hundred years, it was how to negotiate. There was always something that could be bartered. "What is it that you want Kur-Jara?"

The Black Dragon chuckled or growled, Cage couldn't be sure which, and demon dragons sprouted up from the shadows beneath his wings. They surrounded Cage and the two women, pinning them with only the lava to their backs. It shifted into his human form, a man with long dark hair that reminded Cage more of a clichéd vampire than a dragon warrior.

"So, you and your Wyverns brothers have finally learned who I am. I'm a little surprised, seeing as your fathers weren't smart enough to even learn of my existence."

"We know all about you now and how you are the Black Witch's bitch." This guy had the ego the size of hell itself. Any slight would keep him off guard.

"You know nothing. If she and her spells weren't useful to me, I would have roasted her centuries ago."

The Black Witch scoffed from behind them.

"I'll deal with you later, Ereshkigal." The two glared at each other.

The interaction made Cage wonder if they were even working together. He'd remember that and try to use it against them when he could.

"You haven't answered my question. What do you want?" Cage recognized the stalling tactic when he saw it. There was something about the situation that was off for Kur-Jara. The longer he could draw that out, the more time it gave him to come up with a plan.

"I want a lot of things, little golden boy. My birthright, for instance. But, for now I'll be happy with your soul."

Interesting and also nope. "It's not mine to give."

Azynsa owned his soul. He had yet to even claim hers. The tiniest ray of an idea shined into Cage's mind.

"Ah, yes. Your mate. She's given me almost more trouble than she's worth."

A ripple of power burst from behind Cage and Azynsa told the Black Dragon exactly how she felt about that. "Fuck you, asshole. Why don't you call off your guard dogs and come at me like a man for once?"

Yep, that was his mate calling out the Black Dragon like he was some little punk.

What a woman.

"Stop touching her," Kur-Jara snapped.

Cage wasn't touching anyone. Azynsa was though. And there it was. Kur-Jara's problem, the reason he hadn't already tried to take what he wanted from them, what had him so worked up. The woman Azynsa had wanted so badly to save was also important to Kur-Jara. Was she his mate?

Jett's strained voice filtered into Cage's head. *"His daughter."*

What the fuck?

The Black Dragon family tree was sprouting branches all over the place.

Now that was something to negotiate with.

"Why don't we make a deal? Your girl there, for mine."

Both Kur-Jara and Azynsa shouted "no" at the same time.

Cage didn't know what Azynsa's connection was with Kur-Jara's daughter, but he would have to override whatever it was for her safety and freedom.

"Don't you even think about it," she whispered from behind him.

He'd lost his edge if everybody could tell what he was thinking. Fine, on to plan B.

He'd been there when Jakob and Ciara had mated. Both Jakob and Ky had reported that when they first met their mates, their soul shards had glowed, and they had come into more power. Of course, Cage's own mating was all screwed up because he didn't have his soul shard. He had to believe that the results of the process would produce similar effects.

First Dragon, let this work. Because if it didn't, he was only going to piss Kur-Jara off more and not be able to defend himself or Azynsa.

"Sorry, asshole. You're not getting anyone's soul today."

Cage pivoted and pulled Azynsa to him. "Forgive me."

He pushed her hair aside and sunk his teeth into the soft flesh at her neck. Her hands went to his shoulders and gripped him tight. She arched into him, the same way he hoped she would someday soon when he was buried deep inside of her. She moaned low and dug her fingernails into his skin. She tasted of salt and sweet golden honey.

In his mind he thought, "You belong to me and I belong to you. Forever."

A flash of light exploded from the shard at her throat, but only the two of them felt its power.

He released Azynsa's collarbone from his bite and saw pearlescent golden scales ripple across her skin. They traveled along her body, upper arms, and through her fingers onto his shoulders.

She jerked her hand away and scowled at him. Then, she slapped him. There was a litany of unspoken words in her eyes.

He nodded, accepting her rebuke, and said, "That's my girl."

He would apologize for her lack of consent in this plan for the rest of his days. Which made him smile, because he knew now they were going to have many days together. She was his mate, and he was hers.

That changed something deep inside of him and the parts that were missing, that he'd given away for nothing more than sex, were now returned.

The scales solidified and hardened on Cage's skin. With each one he felt a pulse of power pushing into the center of his soul. Hot wind swirled throughout the cavern, whipping through Azynsa's hair. The wind and the power warmed him like sunshine from the inside out, and with a roar he shifted into a great Gold Dragon.

FLIPPING YOUR FINS

*C*age as a dragon was terrifyingly magnificent.

He spread his wings wide and a full-blown tornado whooshed out of them, tossing the demon dragons across the cavern and splatting into walls.

"Grab the girl and go."

Kur-Jara shifted into the Black Dragon and spat a stream of fire toward Cage. He screeched like a giant baby-ass demon dragon when his flames were wrapped up by the tornado and extinguished.

"Not without you." There was no way she could leave him here to sacrifice himself while she got away. That would be too much déjà vu all over again. The Black Dragon was not that much different from a gang leader and Cage was definitely here to serve and protect.

Just like her father had been.

"Dammit, Azynsa, run. I'll be right behind you. There's no getting rid of me now that I have marked and claimed you. You're stuck with me, babe."

Well, all right then. Azy wrapped her arms under Fallyn's shoulders and dragged her, using all of the power in her muscles to make it across the rock floor. She'd never had a problem with the maximus of her gluteus, a.k.a. her big old booty, and she was more than grateful for it right now. She wasn't as strong as a few weeks ago. But, once she was back with the Mami Wata and flipping her fins through the ocean again, she would be back to her old self. Physically anyway.

For the first time since she'd decided to get Fallyn out and the dragons had left her down here, she felt a real glimmer of hope that she might actually get back to the ocean in one piece.

She should have known better.

The entrance to the tunnel was only a few more feet away when Fallyn woke up. She slapped at Azy's hands and twisted her body, trying to get away.

"Fallyn, stop, it's me."

"No, it's not you." She scrambled to her feet and backed away. "I don't know you."

Shit, Azy did not have time for Fallyn's riddles. "You do. Come on, we've got to get away."

That she got. Fallyn took one look in Cage's direction, turned and bolted toward her treasure room. Azy tried to follow, but a demon dragon who'd escaped Cage's tornado dropped from above, landed on her, and pinned her to the ground with its claws. One pierced her shoulder and another her thigh, burning her from the inside out.

Azy gritted her teeth hard rather than cry out. She wouldn't distract Cage in his shootout, or, uh battle with the Black Dragon.

"Get off me, you disgusting piece of shit." She kicked with her other leg and tried to punch it, but the thing held her fast.

The demon dragon sniffed her, drooling as it did, its spittle burned like boiling mucus. "Too late. No good to AllFather."

That was a mouthful and a half for a demon dragon. This one was different—there was an intelligence in its eyes. Maybe she could negotiate with it.

"Let me go and the dragon warrior will spare your life." Probably a lie. It would already be dead if Cage wasn't defending them all against the Black Dragon.

It turned and looked up at Jett, pinned to the ceiling. "No. You help him." It released her arm and grabbed her chin. Help all. Do it."

Help the Black Dragon?

No.

He meant Jett.

The sliced flesh at her leg throbbed as it withdrew its claw. It licked her blood from it then turned and leaped across the room, into the air, toward Cage and the tornado.

Azy couldn't keep quiet this time. "Cage, look out. Behind you."

She clasped her hands over her mouth. A chill, like hell freezing over, washed over her skin and inside. No, no. Not again.

Cage didn't hear her over the din of the wind and battle. The demon dragon was close. Azy tried to get to her feet, but she was losing a lot of blood and her leg wouldn't work. She clasped her hands over the wound. She was not dying in hell, God damn it.

"Cage. Cage." The words were a silent prayer, making no sound, save that of a low keen that escaped from the deepest, darkest part of her heart.

She would not lose him like she'd lost her father. She might not be able to walk, but she could army crawl, or do the 80s worm dance across the floor if she had to. It wasn't that much different than how she used her tail to swim.

Like she even knew how to swim any more. She hadn't been in water or even seen her tail in so long now.

If it was the last thing she did, that demon dragon would not kill Cage. She reached out for him, knowing it was useless but willing him to look at her. Then she grabbed the soul shard she still wore around her neck. It belonged to him, it gave them a connection.

She closed her eyes tight, squeezing them, concentrating on sending him a mental image of the demon dragon headed for his destruction. Cage didn't react, didn't turn or acknowledge her, but a gust of wind brushed against her cheek.

Had she imagined that? No. The wind whipped around her, through her hair and then poof, blew the demon dragon off its course.

Instead of landing on Cage's back, it was caught in the swirling wind.

Yes.

It tumbled, not flailing about like she thought it would but spreading its small wings and riding the storm.

Shit.

Cage was easily in its sights, but it flew right past, tucking its body into an aerodynamic arrow, and shot straight for the Black Witch.

What?

She hadn't moved during the battle, except to press herself to the wall. She kept her tight magical hold on Jett, not letting him fall even an inch from the ceiling.

Had it released her only to assist the Black Witch?

The demon dragon circled the room, riding the wind. On its next pass, it dropped from the swirl of dirt and dust, crashing toward Ereshkigal.

She shrieked, throwing her arms up to block the attack, but she wasn't fast enough to hold back the demon dragon cannon-balling toward her. It crashed into her, rolling across the rock in a tangle of limbs and claws.

Jett, no longer trapped by her spell, dropped from the ceiling, spreading his own wings, and lashed out at the Black Dragon. Cage didn't miss a beat. He blew a new burst of wind that carried Jett past the Black Dragon and right in Azy's direction. Those coal black eyes of Jett's were pissed as hell when he landed beside her.

"I'll get him for that demon dragon's death."

This was war and if Jett wasn't with them, who was he with? She couldn't figure out if he was a good guy or a baddie. "Whose side are you on here?"

"Mine," he growled. He lifted Azy in one of his claws, underneath her legs, and made for the tunnel.

She pushed against him with her uninjured arm, but she was already feeling the effects of her wounds. "We can't leave Cage."

"Fuck me. Don't any of you have any sense of self-preservation."

Jett rolled his eyes, dropped her just inside the tunnel entrance, and turned back to the battle. The Black Dragon had taken to the air and was showering fire down as the pools of lava shot up in spurts. Oh, shit on a shingle. Cage would be caught in the middle.

Jett flew for the ceiling and ran smack dab into a giant stalactite. It and half the rocks in the caldera rained down like hellfire on top of the Black Dragon.

"Get the fuck out of here, gold. That won't keep him long." Jett flew right over Cage's head and into the tunnel, not bothering to stop for Azy this time.

Cage was at her side before she even blinked. He grabbed her up and followed Jett into the darkness.

"Up ahead and to the left is Fallyn's armory. Maybe we can make a stand there."

Cage and Jett followed her directions and in another few flaps of their wings she saw the light coming from the cave where Fallyn had hoarded swords and Christmas ornaments.

Neither were going to do them much good if the Black Dragon came calling. She imagined throwing broken glass bulbs at his face and that made her feel a little better.

Jett went through the cave entrance, and a power like electricity snapped and sparkled across his skin. *"Ouch."*

He landed in a skid and a thud inside the cave. Where he had crossed now sparkled like some kind of force field across the entry to the cave.

Cage pulled up short, landing directly in front of the entry-way. He still cradled Azy in his great claw, holding her away from the power. "She has it shielded somehow."

He sniffed and poked at the energy field at the doorway. *The spell doesn't have an effect on me. But, I'm not going through without you.*

Azy reached her hand out and through the sparkling energy. Where she touched it, the sparkled faded and she felt nothing, just as when she'd gone into Fallyn's cave before. If Jett hadn't crashed through, she wouldn't know any kind of barrier was even there. "I've been in there. I didn't even know there was a spell."

Cage glanced over her shoulder and shoved her into Fallyn's cave, following right behind her.

"I won't have a dragon stealing my hoard." Fallyn stood just inside the entrance, a sword held with the tip pointing at Cage's throat.

A rumble sounded in the tunnel behind them. Jett got to his feet and took a stand in front to the entry, blocking it with his body, his tail poised to strike at anything that came through. A stream of demon dragons ran past the cave, not a one of them even glancing in their direction. They all stayed silent until the final one was gone.

Fallyn was the first one to say anything.

"If you move an inch, I'll push this blade in to your neck. The poison is not for you, but it will hurt in ways you don't even understand."

Cage's eyes grew wide with Fallyn's words, but not in fear—in realization of something important. "You're the one who stabbed Match."

Fallyn spat on the floor.

Yeah. That wasn't the way to get her calmed down. What she needed was a distraction. For that matter, so did Azy. Her wounds were throbbing now. She glanced around the room hoping for inspiration anywhere. Whoop, there it is.

"Ooh. Fallyn, I don't think I remember your ornaments being so, so, brilliant before. Did you do something special to them?"

Fallyn looked over her shoulder toward the display and lowered her sword a few inches.

"The mother gave me a spell to make everything shine like I want."

Interesting, the sparkle around the ornaments echoed the force field. "They're even prettier than before. Is it the same one you used on the entryway to your, uh, treasure cave?"

The sword dropped another few inches. "Ereshkigal doesn't like shiny things. She can't see in here anymore. She gets mad when I don't talk to the mates and takes my things."

Cage stepped away and shifted into his human form but didn't move his gaze from Fallyn and her sword. His change from dragon to man seemed to calm Fallyn and she let the sword drop the rest of the way.

Phew.

He glanced around the room, nodding to Jett to follow suit. "This ward is a powerful spell."

Jett shifted and glared at Fallyn. "Who is the mother?"

Didn't these two know each other? They were both from hell, so Azy assumed they did. She'd kind of wondered if they weren't related somehow since they were the only people down here and weren't actively trying to kill her.

She pressed a hand against the wall to continue to hold herself up. Damn that demon dragon. She would have to ask Jett what the hell was up with it later, when she wasn't so close to throwing up from the pain.

"I think she is mine, or Izzy's. I'm not sure." Fallyn tipped her head in that way that she did when she was thinking about something and glared over at Cage. "She's his mother."

Cage shook his head. "My mom was a human. A beautiful one but nothing more. She had no powers."

Fallyn looked at him like he was stupid or something. "No. Not that one."

Jett circled Fallyn, clearly trying to intimidate her. "Who was this woman? What did she look like?"

Fallyn snarled at him. "She looked like the mother."

"You're not going to get a clearer answer from her than that." Azy was feeling more than a little woozy and these two weren't helping.

"When did she give you this spell?"

Jett was awfully interested in the mother and the spell. Couldn't he give it a rest?

"When the afterlife took the blue dragon warrior."

A giant pit filled with snapping crocodiles opened up in Azy's stomach. "The blue...you mean Ky? Ky didn't die, did he?"

Azy had assumed he'd gotten out with the other dragons. Maybe he hadn't. One more thing she couldn't forgive herself for. Ky Puru had tried to rescue her. Once when she'd been taken by the Black Dragon and his stupid minions in the water cavern and again when he'd been brought down to hell himself.

Cage came up to her and touched his knuckles to her cheek and neck. "No. I was just at his wedding a few weeks ago."

His warmth felt good on her skin. She was cold. For the first time in weeks, she didn't feel the incessant heat of the hellfires. She grabbed his hand and held it to her skin. She tingled everywhere he touched.

Fallyn seemed so far away now. The room had gotten bigger and darker. "Why did you say he was dead?"

"I didn't." Fallyn stared at her and frowned. "Why are you in this place with your dragon, mermaid?"

Oh, to be a mermaid again. Her skin cried out for the cool

waters of the Atlantic. Her scales felt so dry, like she would crack if she went any longer without the sea on her skin.

"Azynsa!"

Her legs went out from underneath her. No, she didn't have legs any longer. She'd lost them. Inch by inch her scales crawled up her skin, fusing her legs together into a tail.

But, those weren't her scales. She was a rich deep yellow, so dark to almost be copper. These scales were brilliant gold, interspersed with pearly white.

That was probably a hallucination. She could tell because everything in the room was wavering and the colors were fading. A muffled buzz went off in her ears.

Aw, crap. She'd lost complete control of her body and she was going to pass out.

Fucking awesome.

Cage grabbed for her, sliding his arms under her tail and supporting her behind the back an instant before she hit the rock floor.

LEGS ARE REQUIRED

*C*age caught Azynsa and lifted her in his arms, holding her tight against his chest. Where her legs would have been, she had a tail, full-on fish fins. It was absolutely gorgeous. Her scales shimmered and shined brighter than any ornament in the room, more than all the gold, coins, jewels, or anything else in his hoard.

This, the most beautiful thing he'd ever seen, and the sight of it had his gut clenching, squeezed by the thought of losing her when he'd only just found her.

"Azynsa, wake up. What's wrong?"

If he wasn't such a dumbass and had been paying attention, he would have seen the wound in her upper right arm seeping blood. Another in her tail looked worse, like a jagged hook had snagged her. Fuck, he should have protected her better. He hadn't even known she'd been hurt.

Her eyelids fluttered open and she grumped at him. "Why do you keep calling me that. Nobody calls me that, except the Mami Wata."

Thank the First Dragon. The fist around his core loosened its grip. She wasn't out of danger yet though. "I'll call you your royal highness supreme, ruler of my universe if you promise never to scare me like that again."

Although, he'd rather call her his lover. This mating had his mind in the gutter when it needed to be on rescuing her.

She blinked a few more times and wriggled in his arms. "I may hold you to that later. Just call me Azy."

Sweet and sassy. He loved it.

"I guess I'm a fish out of water." Azynsa made the joke, but there was real pain in her voice. "I haven't stayed in human form that long since meeting the Mami Wata. I don't really know what happened just now."

Ky knew more about mermaids than he did. He would know better what to do. Cage's own healing abilities were much stronger when he was in dragon form. Perhaps it was the same for other magical beings. "How badly are you hurt?"

The way she bit her lip instead of responding was answer enough. She didn't want to admit any weakness.

Now, that was something Cage could relate to. He may not know much about her, but he wasn't a complete dumbass. She was hot to the touch and her scales and skin were dry.

He turned to Jett and Fallyn. "She needs water."

Jett shrugged. "That's not really a thing in hell."

Azy huffed out a one-note laugh. "That's an understatement."

"Then it's time for us to leave. I've been waiting for you a long ass time. No dying on me now."

"We're not leaving without her." She pointed toward Fallyn.

Fallyn squeaked and backed up until she was surrounded by a circle of swords, and then kept on going until she was hidden behind a whole store worth of Christmas ornaments.

Yeah, that wasn't happening. "I don't think she wants to come with us."

"I'm not leaving without Fallyn."

She was gorgeous, so fierce like this. She was his priority and he wouldn't let anything get in his way of rescuing her. Not even herself.

"You're asking for a shit-ton of trouble. Kur-Jara and Ereshkigal barely let her out of their site, much less leave hell. I didn't sign on for a jailbreak of that magnitude."

"I thought you wanted to cause him trouble."

"Yeah. I do. But, if you take Fallyn out of hell, hell is going to follow. I want to rake that bastard over the coals, but I'm not fucking stupid."

"I'm not going anywhere with a dragon warrior." Fallyn tossed one of her daggers from behind her wall of ornaments, but Cage redirected it to the wall with a breath of wind.

The woman obviously didn't want to go and why would Cage want to help her? She'd attacked and seriously injured Match.

She was important to Azynsa, that's why.

Azy laid her head against his chest and closed her eyes again.

"I can't make her leave if she doesn't want to, love."

"Yes, you can." She swallowed hard, like she was trying not to throw up. "We can't leave her to her father. She's been abused here her entire life. No one should have to live like that."

"Go away." Fallyn hollered from behind her wall of ornaments and threw another dagger.

Cage sidestepped the projectile again. She didn't seem to be trying that hard to actually hit them. "You want us to rescue her from hell."

Azy's face went ashen and her eyes rolled back in her head. She convulsed in his arms. Fuck. Fuck. Fuck.

He was losing her, right here, right now.

The shard at her throat sparked, blinking bright and then off and on again. A sharp emptiness pierced him deep inside. If he didn't get her out of here and god-damned quick he was going to lose her forever.

He knew no help was coming his way, but he sent up a prayer anyway, if only to buoy himself for the upcoming battle to get

Azy safely to the surface. A good warrior had not only brawn, but smarts and knew half of winning any battle was the mental game. "First Dragon, hear my plea. Guide me in the way of your warriors. Show me the way out of here."

The tunnel outside of the cave was empty and looked like the best place to start. With or without Jett and Fallyn, he was taking Azy home. He held her tight in his arms and made for the entryway.

"Izzy says to show you the mermaid's secret."

Cage stopped. Fallyn had come out of her hiding spot. He didn't know who Izzy was, but if she was on his side, then they were about to be new best friends.

"Will the secret help save her?"

Fallyn tipped her head to the side and her eyes flitted from side to side for just a moment. "Yes."

"Then show me."

Fallyn grabbed the mirror Azy had tucked into her belt, the only thing left of the leather leggings she'd been wearing.

"I know. I'm going to. I will. Go away." Fallyn shook her head and rolled her eyes as if they could all commiserate with the frustration she was having over the conversation with the person in her head.

It sure as hell didn't seem like a good idea to follow a crazy person through the tunnels of hell, though he didn't exactly have another choice at the moment.

"Lead on."

Fallyn redirected her eye roll at him. She held up the mirror so that he was looking directly into it. Only his own reflection did not look back at him.

"You're the one connected to the mermaid. Not me, anymore." She seriously thought Cage was a dumbass.

He stared into the mirror again and saw a cave with water dripping into it from above. "Where is this?"

Jett folded his arms and scowled. "What do you see?"

"Rocks, dirt, nothing that seems any more indistinguishable than where we're standing now. Except for the water."

Azynsa stilled in his arms, unconscious but not seizing anymore.

"Ask her." Again, with the don't be stupid tone. "You're in her head and she's the only one who knows where to go."

He didn't feel like he was that deeply connected to her. He'd only just marked and claimed her. She owned his soul, and he knew at a visceral level that they belonged together. He didn't know her well enough to understand what she was thinking.

He liked to pretend he knew women, but he knew only their bodies, what turned them on.

Beyond that they were as mysterious to him as mermaids.

He did know to play to his strengths. That was what made him a good warrior in the first place.

Cage lifted Azy's back and brought her head up to his. She had such plump lips and all he could think was "mine."

He brushed his lips across hers, feeling how rough and dry they were. He dipped his tongue out wetting them both. "Azynsa, my mate. I know you're in there and I think you can hear me. Let me in, my love."

She released a soft sigh and the image in the mirror lit up brightly enough to draw his attention away from her lips.

The droplets of water shimmered with a yellow-gold light that matched the spark of his soul shard. They pooled on the floor of a small cave. The view changed, as if Azy were looking up. The water was falling from leaves and a small root poking through the dirt of the ceiling.

That was the only bit of life Cage had seen since they had entered the caldera and began their descent through the gates of hell.

The water and the light inside of it pulsed with elemental magic. She was giving him every clue she could.

He pressed a real kiss to her lips this time. "That's my girl."

Jett had been with Jakob and Kai down here in hell before. He knew how they escaped and where. "The escape route Jakob carved through the stone. That's where her secret hideout is."

"Smart girl," Jett said.

"Can you lead us there?"

"Yeah, but I can't guarantee there won't be a horde of demon dragons crawling all over it."

Fallyn sniffed and made a face at Jett. "Tell them to go away."

Was she simply rambling again? Cage thought not. "You can communicate with them, can't you? Control them even."

What a bastard. Jett was more than just a rogue dragon. When they were safely out of hell, he and Jett were having a serious conversation.

"I don't control them. But, they are my brethren. Some of them will listen to me. The ones that don't aren't worth saving."

There was too much going on here that Cage did not have time to interpret. Jett had fought against and slaughtered his fair share of demon dragons while they had been down here. If he would continue to do that, the rest didn't matter to Cage. Only getting Azy to safety did. "Then, I expect you to use that advantage to help me save my mate now."

"I will, golden boy. But, don't forget that favor you owe me. It's getting bigger by the minute."

Azy whimpered softly. The image in the mirror shifted and Cage now saw Fallyn. She was chained to a rock. No, she was gripping the chains. A whip of fire sliced through the air behind her and into her back. Her mouth moved saying the number eleven but without any sound.

Shit. That favor he owed Jett was about to get a lot bigger.

"I will do whatever it is you require. Now grab the girl and let's go."

Jett raised one eyebrow but nodded. He stalked toward Fallyn. She dropped the mirror, but Jett caught it and her. She screamed and thrashed in his arms until Jett wrapped his arm around her neck and pinched her in a full on Vulcan death grip. She collapsed, and he hefted her up and over his shoulder.

"Let's go."

He shoved the mirror back through Azy's belt and then nodded, ready to move out.

Jett pushed through the entryway first, the shield zapping him again. "Ouch, God dammit."

Cage pushed through with Azy in his arms and didn't feel a thing. "Which way?"

This part of the tunnel was so dark it sapped Cage's energy just by being in it. The only light was from the glowing shard nestled against her skin.

Jett was clearly comfortable in the pitch black because he took off down the tunnel. The black dragon's nature was still so unknown to him. Despite being a pretty big dickhead, Cage kinda, sorta, wanted to like the guy. Yeah, he had his own agenda and the way he went about accomplishing it had made trouble for Cage and the other dragon warriors, but the goal was the same. Defeat the Black Dragon.

He still couldn't completely be trusted. A few more battles where he proved himself like back there in the cavern would help though.

Not like Cage was looking forward to running into demon dragons or their leader.

That was a first for him. His entire life up until he'd been struck down by the loss of his shard had been about three things. Treasure, sex, and being a warrior.

His father would be horrified if he found out that Cage couldn't give a flying fuck about his treasure. Azynsa was the only treasure he needed.

The possessiveness he felt about her would probably piss her off.

For the first time, Cage found himself wary of fighting a

battle. Normally, it was just as fun as sex and had kept him going when his libido had flagged.

Cage wanted nothing to do with anything that would take him and his attention away from being with Azy. She moaned as he carried her across the ground.

The jostling had set the wound in her arm to bleeding again. "Shush, shush, shush. I've got you. Hang on for me."

He picked up his pace, pushing Jett from behind to hurry. Jett slowed down.

"The place where your friends escaped isn't far. The way is blocked by a horde of demon dragons up ahead."

Cage didn't see or hear anything.

"They haven't sensed us yet. Their attentions are divided."

They had only two choices. Find a way around or fight through them.

"There is no other route. Only one tunnel passes by this hiding place of hers. I don't know how they haven't found it yet."

Shit. "Then we fight our way through. Unless you can persuade them to back down."

Undoubtedly, it would not be that easy.

Jett stopped before a turn in the tunnel. "I might be able to, if we didn't have Fallyn. I tried to tell you, he will never let her go."

If Cage had any idea where he was going, he would shift into his dragon form and carry both women away. He didn't see how anyone could find their way around this maze in the dark as it was.

They were between the dark and a hard place.

It was getting darker by the moment.

The hissing and screeches of the demon dragons became a cacophony in front of them. The bastards began popping up all around them.

Cage and Jett retreated until their backs were at each other. "If you've got any sway now would be the time to use it."

Jett snarled at the closest demon dragons.

They had nowhere to run, nowhere to hide. It was about kill or be killed.

There was no way he could allow them to harm Azy. She had already willingly sacrificed her own wellbeing for Fallyn's for long enough.

"What do you think I've been doing? If it weren't for me they would already have killed you and your mate and probably taken me prisoner."

He hissed and growled again, and this time Cage realized two big demon dragons at the front of the pack were replying in kind.

"What are they saying?"

Jett half laughed. "They say I can go, if I give them you and the mermaid."

Great. "I'm afraid our deal will be null and void if I die here and now."

"No shit. We have to give them something to take back to Kur-Jara. They know better than to return emptyhanded and say that we've escaped."

Cage had very little to give. The sword from the First Dragon, Azy's mirror, and his pants. That was all he had left. Except himself.

He'd known since Azy first touched his soul shard that he would give his own life for hers. What he wanted more than anything else in the world was to spend the rest of his life learning to love her, be the man, the dragon she deserved. That may not be what she needed.

He knew very little about the mating habits of either dragons or mermaids. He suspected that neither would mate again. Hopefully, he was wrong, and she could find another.

He glanced down at Azy's round cheeks and luscious lips. Even in the dark he could see she was even paler than before. He pressed a kiss to her forehead, not trusting himself to give her anything more, knowing he was only going to take it away again forever. "Please, forgive me."

A shard could only be given, never taken.

He knew that better than anyone.

"Azynsa, wake up, love."

She moaned and her eyes fluttered open.

"That's my girl. Will you give me the shard?"

Her eyes were tired and unfocused. "It's yours."

He lifted the shard from her neck and pulled the cord over her head, then slipped it over his again.

"What Kur-Jara really wants is me and my soul. Tell them they can have it if they let you and the women go."

The demon dragons must have understood what he was saying, because they crept closer and hissed and clacked their teeth at him.

"Don't be a dumbass. Didn't we just decide I don't get my favor if you die?"

Cage turned and lifted Azy to hand her over to Jett. "Gris already has instructions on what to do in the event I don't return. Take Azy to him and you'll get whatever you want."

Jett shook his head in that way that meant he still thought Cage's plan was stupid but would go along with it.

Cage might be going to his doom willingly, however, he wasn't going to make it easy for the little fuckers. He knew he had enough light in him to blast at least the first dozen or so into dust. More would fall to his teeth, claws, and tail before they took him down. Were they on the surface, with even a setting sun, he could take out at least half of them. The darkness had taken its toll on his soul and his powers.

Before he could hand her over, Azy reached her hand up and clasped the soul shard. "Don't even think about it, dragon. This is mine."

Her voice was weak and thready and still brooked no argument.

"All will be well, my little mermaid. Jett will get you back to your people or mine, whichever you choose."

She blinked like the words coming out of his mouth didn't make any sense. After a deep breath, she got a second wind, all of which she blew at him. "I'm not some Disney princess. I'm a fierce fucking mermaid, and if you die on me now, I will kill you."

"Azy." They didn't have another choice. She had to see that.

Or not.

A demon dragon reached out and she flicked it with her tail hard enough to send it scurrying back into the horde.

"Don't you Azy me. I am tired, I am thirsty, I am god-damned bleeding, and I have had just about enough of everybody's shit."

Nope. She definitely didn't see.

Another demon dragon hissed and moved closer.

"Bring it, motherfuckers. I will bitch slap you into next week with my tail if I have to."

Jett nodded toward the demon dragons, who were again advancing but this time as a group. "I suggest you start doing exactly that, because we've dicked around long enough. Kur-Jara is coming."

Shit on a shingle on a shit brick house.

AZYNSA IN WONDERLAND

*N*othing like a little mad to get the ole adrenaline pumping. Azy was fucking pissed, so there was a huge surge running through her veins at the moment.

Cage, who was supposed to be her mate, thought he could come all up in here, try to rescue her and then sacrifice himself to save her. Uh…how about no.

Hells to the no.

A lot of her strength had returned. Would have been nice if any of the other Mami Wata had given her the heads up that her mermaid form helped her heal faster. Maybe they didn't know. Not like anyone else she knew was half-human.

Sure, they used their human-like forms when they mated, but that never made them weaker. She guessed it didn't make them any more human than they were either.

Azy concentrated and visualized her own legs shifting back, but they simply wouldn't come out to play. She was going to need them for strolling along down the…what's that word again… stain of black demon dragon death.

She was still no little mermaid. She was a big, black, beautiful, bootyliscious Mami Wata who was going to kick some faces in.

As soon as she got her feet back.

Barring that, she needed a weapon and a partner in crime, not a sacrificial lamb. She yanked the mirror out of her belt. "Do that trick with your light again."

Fallyn groaned, waking up. "Izzy says use the mirror, mermaid. The warrior has the sword. I told her to shut up."

Use the mirror? That's what she was trying to do.

Cage brought up the ball of light and held it up to the mirror. This time it didn't reflect back. The mirror was black. Great time for a defective mermaid mirror.

"I was prepared to die for you," he said.

Azy grabbed his chin and kissed him once, hard. "Yeah. Don't do that. I'd have to kick your ass for even thinking about something so friggin' stupid."

"I'd rather fight for you, anyway. More fun." He winked at her and threw that ball of light at the approaching demon dragons. They recoiled and hissed.

Jett rolled his eyes at them. "Do either of you two have a fucking plan here, or are we fighting with the power of love?"

Christ. Azy wasn't in love with Cage. Yet. But, she sure as shit would like the chance to fall for him.

Fallyn kneed Jett in the chest and he almost dropped her. "Stop telling me what to do."

"No one is talking to you." Jett readjusted his hold on her. "I'm going to drop this crazeball on her ass in another second."

Whoever the voice in Fallyn's head was, she knew things the rest of them didn't. "Fallyn, how does Izzy want me to use the mirror?"

"Duh. Go through it."

"Like Alice?"

"Who is Alice?"

She kneed Jett in the chest again and he did drop her this time. "Dammit, Fallyn. These people are trying to save your crazy ass. Quit fighting us."

Fallyn stood, hissed at the demon dragons who'd gotten a little too close for comfort and glared at them with her fire eyes. They backed off.

Smoke billowed up behind them and they advanced again. Flames liked along the wall, announcing their enemy's arrival

The Black Dragon stomped around the corner, swishing his tail back and forth, obliterating the walls. Demon Dragons jumped out of his way, opening the path directly to their band of not so merry men.

Okay. Awesome. Now what? "How do we go through the mirror?"

"She's not going to help you. Say your prayers, kids. We're all about to die in a blaze of glory." Jett shifted into his dragon form and spewed fire at the Black Dragon.

Fallyn rolled her eyes, not the least bit afraid or bothered by anything. She grabbed Azy's hand that held the mirror.

"Where's your secret mirror?"

"You're holding it."

"The one you contacted your warrior with," Fallyn glared at Cage, "his reflection."

She'd seen Cage twice in a mirror. The Christmas ornament and in the droplet of water in her hideout. "The reflection in the water droplet?"

The image of her little cave appeared in the mirror.

"Yes." Fallyn yanked Cage's sword away from him. He lunged for it, clasping the hilt just below hers. He wasn't fast enough to stop Fallyn from thrusting it toward Jett's big scaly ass. The tip pierced him between two of the scales and he roared out.

One second his dragon's fire filled the tunnel, the next he was gone in a puff of mist. His roar could still be heard, but it was muffled and coming from inside the mirror.

"Holy shit. He went through the mirror," Cage said.

Fallyn released both of them and clapped her hands. "Ha ha ha. Me next."

She pointed the tip of Cage's sword at her chest, stuck her tongue out the demon dragons, and stepped forward into the blade.

Poof.

"Ow. Get off me."

"Mermaid, this place is too small. You should find a bigger cave to hide in."

Jett and Fallyn's muffled arguing came through the mirror. God, she was right. Azy barely felt comfortable in that little hole in the rock—all four of them were going to crush each other.

"Bring her back or I will hunt you to the ends of the universe and make you pay," the Black Dragon roared into their heads.

"Time to go. Ladies first." Cage grabbed her hand and pointed the tip of the sword toward her palm.

"Wait, no. We go together."

Cage nodded. "Better together."

He boosted her in his arm, letting her tail dangle, kissed her hard and fast, and sliced the blade across their shoulders at the same time.

The world went wonky and wet like they were doing cartwheels through one of those mist spraying machines at a theme park on a hot day in the middle of summer.

In the next second, they were slamming their backs against the dirt and stone in her hidden cave. Rocks tumbled down all around them, piling on top of what looked like a landslide over the tiny crack she usually slipped through to get in and out.

"For fucks sake, get off of me."

Jett shoved them, and Cage moved forward a whole five or six inches. He still held Azy in his arm, but her feet touched the ground under them. Her feet.

"Yes. Finally." She wiggled her toes and stretched her legs. The gashes in her thigh and arm were still raw but weren't bleeding.

"That's some magic mirror," Cage said. Their bodies were

smashed together, front to front, and Azy could feel every blessed inch of his hard, honed body.

His shard was hanging around his neck, right in front of her face. It felt strange to not be wearing it after all these days. She didn't feel its loss though. Somehow, even though she wasn't wearing it, she could still feel the connection between them.

It was different now. She couldn't describe how. Like a warm current that pulled her closer to him and him to her.

She dragged her gaze up from his entirely too naked chest to his golden eyes. God, they were actually gold. Not sparkly brown or some indescribably hazel, but twenty-four carats.

He stared right back at her with an intensity that made her feel like she could see straight into her head, where she kept all the totally inappropriate thoughts about just what she'd like to do to all his half naked-ness. Or his whole nakedness.

"If you guys are going to make out, I'm shifting and busting through these rocks."

Cage waited one more moment before he cleared his throat and looked over her head to Jett behind her. "Feel free to bust on out of here. If you've got any idea how or where to go."

"Mermaid. This adventure has been, umm, weird. But, I'd like to go back to my shiny hoard now."

Azy tried to twist to see Fallyn, but she was fully wedged between the rock and Cage's hard place. "I don't think I can do that."

"Just use one of my...what did you call them? Oh, ornaments to reflect through. The sooner the better, I am not enjoying having my face smashed into dragonling's armpit."

No, one wouldn't.

"Can I use it to reflect us up to the surface?"

Fallyn gasped. "No no no no no no no no no no no no no. I don't go up there. There are dragons up there."

"Dumb bunny, there are dragons in here," Jett said.

"What? Where? Don't let them see me. Dragons are evil.

They're trying to kidnap me and take me to their red devil leader. Get me out of here." Fallyn screeched and Jett let out a yelp.

"You've got about ten seconds to magic us out of here before I do more permanent damage to the crazeball's brain. She's clawing the shit out of me."

Cage pulled Azy tighter to him, protecting her back with his arms. "She's your sister, dude."

"She's not my brethren." He yelped again, and rocks tumbled down from the top of the cave where he was trying to claw his way out.

Azy scooched her arm up and around and looked into the mirror. First, she saw Fallyn's cave and didn't want to go back there again. Then the view changed, and she was looking at a spot a good hundred miles off shore where she and some of the other Mami Wata went to sun themselves on the rocks. Yes, that would work.

She blinked, and the view changed again to the bedroom of the house where she'd grown up. The room was painted a different color and there were posters of Pokémon and dinosaur toys spread across the floor, but that was definitely her room. She could see it as clearly as if she were standing in the doorway.

There had been a mirror on the back of her door. Yes, that was exactly where she stood. She could see the street and the neighbor's yard out of the window.

The memories of that old room in a house she hadn't seen in five years hit her harder in the gut than a bullet. She swallowed past the lump in her throat willing that sight away.

The mirror darkened, allowing her to breathe again. She thought it was finished showing her reflections, but then she noticed the motion of a blue-scaled tail swish by just along the edge. Yes, there was a tiny trail of bubbles and then another glimpse of scales. Only these ones were bigger and distinctly un-mermaid like.

"What do you see?" Cage's voice bubbled up through the filter of the images in the mirror.

"I think it shows me reflections of places I've been. Or maybe mirrors I've looked into before. I'm not sure what it's showing me now, but I think it's the reflection of another Mami Wata's mirror."

"There are more of these?"

"All Mami Wata have mirrors. Except me. They are passed down from mother to daughter, but my mother's mirror was lost. Or so they told me."

Jett grumbled and tried to move the rocks around them again. "If you can see someplace else, get us the fuck out of here."

"I don't think you want to go where I'm seeing right now. Unless you know how to breathe underwater."

"I'll learn."

"No no no no no no no no. I'll melt. Take me back to my cave."

The blue tail moved again and now Azy had a clear view of the other scaled creature. "Ky Puru."

"Shit. I was trying to keep him out of this."

Ky Puru and the Mami Wata whose mirror Azy was looking out of were saying something, but she couldn't hear Ky.

"Shush your faces, you two, I'm trying to hear."

Azy strained to catch any words. "We'll send someone right away if we see anything."

Ky Puru nodded and swam away, toward the surface.

"If Ky is here, you should go through the mirror to him. We'll figure out how to dig our way out of here if we have to." Cage wiggled the sword, but there was no room to lift it.

The water did look delicious and cool. "Yeah, no. I'm not just leaving you three down here to see whose claustrophobia kicks in first. We go together, or we don't go at all."

"You're as fucking stubborn as I am." Cage grinned down at her. "If prude boy over there wasn't so squeamish I'd have my way with you right here and now."

Jett shifted, trying to put any sort of space between them. "Dear God. Burn me now."

"I can't control the visions on the mirror. They keep changing. I don't know where we'd end up. There has to be another way out of here.

"We already know we work better together. Let's put our heads together and figure out our next move."

Fallyn started shouting in corner. "Ow. Ow. Ow. Why is there water dripping on me. I'm going to die."

"Water? My root!" Azy wriggled her way down Cage's body, passing an impressive package and promising to return to that later. She scooted along the cave floor, under everyone's legs and then worked her way back up between Fallyn and Jett.

"Whoa, hey. I'm saying right here and now, I am not touching your mate in any way that's inappropriate. She's the one whose got her ass all up in my junk."

Cage growled and the sword he couldn't figure out how to get out earlier smacked the rock above his head.

Azy ignored their bro show and reached above Fallyn's head, stopping the next droplet from hitting her. It ran down her finger and soaked into her parched skin.

"God, yes." She moaned as another drop hit her skin and she brought it to her mouth. "Mmm."

"Christ on cracker, woman. Those moans. Are you trying to get me killed?"

"Azynsa." Cage's voice was harsh and dark.

"Hakuna your tatas, fellas. I think I found our way out." Her little root has sprouted tiny green leaves that crawled across the ceiling. "Cage, you got any of that sunshine left?"

"Yeah." He sounded relieved.

"Shoot it on over here. This little guy is going to break us out."

AIN'T NO SUNSHINE

Finally, something he could do that didn't involve a rock jabbing into his asscrack. Cage mustered up the remaining energy he had from the sun and spun it into a ball. He'd been underground far too long, and this would be the last of the light he had to give. Hopefully, it did what Azy thought it would and get them out of hell once and for all.

The light pooled in his hand and he gave it a light puff of air to send it on its way. It crept across the ceiling, lighting up the dirty cave like rays poking through the dark clouds.

The instant it hit the tiny pale leaves Azy had found, they burst open and grew the size of elephant ears. She whispered encouragement to the plant that made him chuckle even as he had to press himself against the wall to stay upright.

"They need more. Sun and water."

Crap. Cage reached deep inside, found the spark of life that kept him going and slowly drew it out. It was all he had left so if this didn't work, they'd be on their own.

No. Azy wouldn't allow that. The thought of how pissed she'd gotten when he'd tried to sacrifice his life for hers added strength to the light, both inside him and to the sunshine imbuing life into this dark corner of hell.

She didn't want him to die for her. What else could he do but as she wished.

"It's drying out. It needs more water." Azy caressed one of the leaves and part of it broke off in her hand.

"That I can't help you with, love."

"Use your own elemental power, mermaid," Fallyn said. "No, wait, pretend I didn't say that. Shut up. No, you shut up."

Huh. Did mermaids have power over water like blue dragons? Why hadn't Azy used her ability all along?

"If I could, don't you think I would have been hot tubbing it up down here? Only witches and blue dragons can call to the water and ask it to bend to their will. I am neither."

Well, that answered that question.

Fallyn squawked again. "I'm not telling her that. No. There is no such thing as... Shut. Up."

In a voice like a stern schoolmarm Azy questioned the woman. "Fallyn, what did Izzy say?"

"Nothing."

"Fallyn. I'll drop water on your head if you don't tell me."

"Ack. You have the power. If you didn't you would have died down here within the first day."

Azy open-mouth stared at Fallyn. "You could've told me this days ago."

"I didn't know." Fallyn shrank away.

"I'm getting a cramp in my I-don't-care. Just get us the fuck out of here." Jett grumbled and tried to readjust his big frame in the small space, which of course made rocks and dirt rain down on their heads.

Azy kicked Jett in the shin. "Shut your pie hole while I try to figure this out."

She reached up and through the leaves, gently pulling the

stalk and root toward her. She bit her lip and glanced over at Cage.

He did his best to look at her like he wasn't about to pass out and gave her a wink. He had about ten more seconds of light to give her. "You got this. I know little to nothing about how water works but with the wind and sun I only have to hold it in my mind and ask it to do what I need. For those that have the power over the element, you can bend it to your will."

"I am not down with the whole power over and bending it to my will bit. We are having a discussion about those two things later, dragon."

If there was a room in here, Cage thought she would be waggling her finger at him like an angry schoolmarm. Apparently, he had a thing for the sexy teacher thing with her.

"Everyone has their own relationship with the elements, you have to find yours with it. But, you need to do it fast, because I've used up every reserve of energy I had to give you that sunlight. It's the light of day or bust for me."

"Shit! Stupid stoic males." Her face crinkled into a look of determination and she gave him a quick silent nod. She closed her eyes and cupped the root in her palm. "Dear water element."

The words fell out of her mouth in unsure somersaults.

Jett snorted, but before he could say anything about Azy's form of incantation, Cage kicked him in the other shin.

Azy started again. "Dear water element, please ignore the males in the room, and their dumbassery. Let's show them who's in charge here, together. Please help this little plant grow into a great big one that can break open the earth with the power your life-giving element grants it. Thank you very much."

They all stared at the root and waited. The sunlight swirling around it flickered and faded. Cage took several deep breaths and called upon his dragon to keep him conscious. If he could hold out a little longer, he was sure her plan would work, and he'd be flying into the sun or the moon in no time.

He gritted his teeth and forced his eyes to stay open.

Jett shook his head. "Yeah, that didn't work. I don't think the elements respond to niceties."

"Ha ha ha. Boy, are you wrong, dragonling." Fallyn crouched down as far as she could and covered her head with her arms.

A rumbling came from somewhere above them. Little drips of water rained down around the root and leaves. Then rocks and other debris fell in a slurry of mud.

Cage shoved his hand between the rock and Jett, grabbing Azy's arm.

Good thing he did too because in the next instant they were both dragged up into a crevasse that was growing by the second, pushed open by water, plant, and magic.

"Holy Mary, mother of ack –" Azy's words were cut off, but Cage knew exactly what she meant.

Rocks and boulders and debris showered down and around them. He blocked as many as he could from hitting Azy. The farther they traveled upward, the wider the space in the earth became. A huge chunk of earth tremored above them. There was no dodging that metric ton of rock.

"Look out. Go, go." Behind them Jett shifted into his dragon form and had snagged Fallyn in his talons. He flapped his wings and overtook them.

Cage did the same and wrapped Azy in his claws. He twisted and turned, asking the wind to push his flight and keep the debris at bay until they were passed. A warm Zephyr of wind whooshed over them, pushing all four of them up like rockets, out of the earth and into the sky.

The sun was just rising over the horizon and Cage continued their assent, soaking up every last molecule of energy and vitamin D from the sun.

"Oh my God, oh my God. What are you doing? Take us down, right now. Unless, you want me to throw up all over you. Because I will." Azy wrapped her arms around his foreleg and clung to him. Her body shivered, and it wasn't from the cool morning air.

She was fucking afraid of heights.

A fish and a bird could fall in love, but where would they live?

"Cage. You take me down right now." There wasn't a wobble in her voice. She knew exactly what she wanted.

"*It's all right, babe. I got you.*"

"You'd better."

Below them, where the earth had opened up, he could see a little oasis, with a pool of water and if he wasn't mistaken a tree of Hesperides mixed in among the native trees and bushes. He headed for the oasis in a long circular descent. He figured that would scare Azy less than a divebomb.

He hated the way she shook and pulled warmth from the sun around her like a blanket.

"You love the sky, don't you?"

"*Yes.*" He wasn't sure what else to say. Was she expecting him to try and show her the beauty of writing crisp currents, being able to see the curve of the earth?

"I'll be okay, if you want to take your time." The only thing that betrayed her lie was the death grip she had on his leg.

He wanted to kiss her for it. He hadn't ever kissed a woman while flying. His brain exploded with visions of a whole new kind of mile high club.

Not with her shaking and fearful.

Now that they had escaped hell, his first order of business was to properly claim his mate in every way that he could. Which meant getting to ground as soon as possible.

Cage folded in his wings and tucked Azy tight against his belly.

"What are you do oh oh oh oh –"

Cage streaked toward the ground and hummed a tune, a very old lullaby, just for his mate. He scanned the ground for any sign that the Black Dragon and his minions had followed them. So far, he saw nothing. This place, this little oasis had some powerful magic, and he let that power sink into him. Safety, respite, and a little bit of…lust, floated through his senses. This place was not merely a natural phenomenon. The elemental powers and magic of dragons was here. Good. Finally, something in this day was going right.

"Please don't crash, please don't crash, please don't crash."

He could see how she thought they were going to ram into the trees, but he was a better flyer than that. He unfurled his wings once again, catching the air like a parachute, and then drifted softly to the ground.

"*Azy, you can open your eyes now.*"

"Are we dead?" She didn't open her eyes and didn't release her grip on him. Her knees were tucked up next to her chin, which had her plump bum curled into his claw. He liked the feel of that. He'd like to have his human hands on her ass even more.

"*No. I don't think so,*" he teased.

She pried one eye open and glanced around. The other eye followed. One arm tentatively reached out and when her fingers touched the ground, Cage felt her entire body relax.

"Thank goodness." She tumbled out of his grasp and stood. "Where are Jett and Fallyn? They made it out too, didn't they?"

"*I'm sure they did. I am more concerned about you than them right now.*" He lowered his head and snuffled at her injuries.

She smacked him on the snout. He wasn't having any of that. He snuffled her again, this time at her neck, pushing her head to the side so he could get access to the mark he'd left on her. He knew it was here somewhere, he could sense it, scent it, practically taste it. She was his and the whole world would know.

"Stop that. What are you doing?" She tried to push his snout away, but he would not be swayed.

"*Looking for your mark.*" Hmm, maybe he'd bitten her on the other shoulder.

"My what?" She had stopped resisting him and let him pull

the tattered remains of the shirt away from her shoulders with his teeth.

"Your mark. When I claimed you I marked your shoulder, I bound us together and placed my mark on your skin. You are mine and any other dragon will know it."

Aha. Once he had her shirt pushed away, the gold dragon tattoo glowed on her skin. He couldn't imagine anything more beautiful than the look of liquid gold across her brown skin. He swiped his dragon's tongue across the mark and shifted into his human form, replacing the rough scales with his lips.

"I am adding that misogynistic attitude about belonging to you to my list of things were going to talk about. But, later because damn, that feels really fucking good and I don't want you to stop."

Cage chuckled and followed the pattern of the mark from her neck across her shoulder and then traced the path of the tail to where it disappeared beneath the leather.

"Oh, yeah. Right there. I don't understand how my clavicle got to be an erogenous zone, but I'm down with that. Wait, are we safe? Are demon dragons going to interrupt this celebration?"

"We are safe. The earth has collapsed back over the gap and the magic of this oasis is stronger than the ward on Fallyn's treasure trove."

"Sweet." She grabbed him by the collar and mashed her mouth to his. Her tongue darted into his mouth and her salty flavor exploded into him. "Wait. Did you say oasis?"

Cage sucked her lip into his mouth and mumbled, "Mmm-hmm."

Azy wrapped one leg around the back of his calf, pulling their centers together. "Like with a pool?"

"Yes. I believe it is a spring." Which she needed to be in right now. Cage ran his hand over Azy's thigh and then lifted her up so she straddled him. This was rapidly becoming his favorite place in the whole wide world to be. Between her legs.

She put her arms around his neck and dipped her head to nibble at his ear. The woman's lips were like magic, sending shots of pure desire through his system.

He took long strides, headed in the direction he saw the water from the sky. It couldn't be more than a few hundred meters from where he landed.

Yes, there, up ahead, the water gleamed in the morning sunlight, throwing a reflection of sparkles into the air around it like a mirage. A mirage that looked strikingly like a woman standing next to the pool's edge.

"You know I can breathe underwater, right?" Azy's voice had gone husky and seductive.

Was she hinting at what she wanted to do to him in said water? Fuck, yeah.

"Hello, my lord Gylden. I see you retrieved your mate."

Cage stopped dead in his tracks. God dammit. As much as he had wanted it to be, the figure at the water's edge wasn't a mirage. It was a beautiful young woman in a gold toga.

Azy froze in his arms. All except her head and neck, which turned to stare at the woman.

"Azynsa." The woman in gold nodded. "I'm glad to see you returned to the land of the living. We were worried about you for a while there. Hell is no place for a creature of the water, like you."

"No shit, Sherlock. Who are you?"

Two more women rushed over and joined the lady in gold. At least he knew who these ones were. Ciara and Jada, mates of his brother Wyverns.

"Ninsy. We told you to wait until they'd had their sexy times." Jada grabbed the woman's arm and tried to drag her away.

"My apologies, my lord, my lady. I merely wanted to let you know my mistress sent me to assist you and that Fallyn is safe with us now. Please," she motioned to the water, "carry on."

Much to Cage's chagrin, Azy slid her legs down and stepped

away from him. He grabbed her hand, not letting her get too far away.

"Uh, thanks. But, I'm not much into exhibitionism." Azy widened her eyes at the rest of them, saying with her expression that the whole lot of them needed to skedaddle.

"Oh, god. Sorry. We'll leave you two alone." Ciara grabbed the Ninsy woman's other arm and gave it a tug. "But, when you're done, come find us. We've got so much to talk about now that you're a Wyvern's mate too."

"A whosie whatsie now?"

Jada waved them toward the water. "We totally get the whole mating lust thing, so take your time. But, when you need refreshments, I've got coffee and donuts in my tent. If Ky hasn't eaten them all yet."

Azy looked from him to the women and back. Cage almost wanted to laugh out loud. She was so completely torn.

"Come on, let me feed you. Jada does make the most sinful pastries in the world." He squeezed her hand and led her after the women. "When you've had your fill, then it will be my turn to eat."

"Don't tell me you're one of those health nuts that doesn't eat sugar or something. Because that might be a deal breaker for me."

"I'm sure you'll be just as sweet as any dessert."

Azy laughed out loud. It was the first time he'd ever heard her do that, and the sound went straight to his cock.

"You're dirty, dragon."

Fuck. Maybe they could take a quick dip in the spring.

No. He had to feed and care for her. Her wellbeing was his main priority. His dick wasn't happy about taking second place, but a little anticipation never hurt anyone.

He would spend the next hour or so imagining all the ways he was going to make her come.

"Yes, I am, mate. I'm very much looking forward to being as

dirty as possible with you." He stepped in line, following the women to wherever they were preparing food.

He'd have a good long chat with Jakob and Ky, make sure Fallyn was being taken care of, see what kind of favor Jett wanted, and follow up with Gris and Zon.

See, he had lots of things to take his mind off stripping Azy naked and licking her from top to bottom. Mmm. Her luscious bottom. God, she had a great ass.

Shit. There went his dick twitching again.

Cage went all of two steps and Azy hadn't taken one. He gave her hand a tug. Maybe she was nervous about spending time with the other Wyvern's mates. She didn't need to be—they were great.

"Az? Everything okay?" He'd assumed her injuries were healed. The adrenaline of their escape and flight were fading from his own system, so they likely were from hers too. She'd be feeling any injuries. He would get Jakob to heal her with his Dragon's breath.

"You're going the wrong way."

"I'm just following…" Azy still had his hand in hers and was caressing the back of his with her thumb.

The look on her face said it all. Donuts can wait, dumbass.

HUNGRY

Starving. Until now that was only a casual word in Azy's vocabulary.

Back when she lived in Illinois, she and her friends had hit the mall food court when they were sure they were starving. When she'd first come to live with the Mami Wata and had to learn how to catch her own dinner, she'd been hungry as all get out for the first few days. The past weeks spent literally in hell where she'd eaten only a handful of times, she was sure she'd learned the true meaning of the word.

None of those experiences with an empty stomach even compared to the deep need and hollowness she felt inside right now.

The moment her brain caught up with her body knowing that they were out of danger, at least for now, and in a safe place, her appetite for all things Cage had exploded.

"The donuts can wait. I can't." She had no doubt she was not good at flirting. It wasn't like she had a lot of experience at it. Cage standing there slack-jawed was not the response she had been trying to elicit.

He had demonstrated quite a bit that the alpha male part of

him ruled his world. Maybe he wasn't used to having a woman come on to him, or initiate sex.

For one fleeting moment she worried that she had it all wrong and Cage didn't want her that way.

Nah. She knew an erection when she felt one in his pants.

Azy tugged Cage to her and cupped his cheek and chin, intending to pull him in for a kiss. That would leave little doubt in his mind what she wanted. It wasn't like she was hinting at getting busy with him in the first place, but sometimes guys were dumb and needed it spelled out for them. She would spell it in body language.

"I thought you were hungry." His gaze flicked from her lips to her eyes.

She had to give him a lot of credit for trying to keep it in his pants when he thought she wanted him to. "I am, for you."

"Are you sure? Jada does make really good donuts and I'm sure you didn't exactly get three square meals a day down in hell."

She wanted to kiss him just for trying to be a good guy. She was going to kiss him because if she didn't, he was never going to shut up. Azy licked her lips and loved how his eyes were fixated on her mouth.

"A minute ago, you couldn't keep your hands or your tongue off me. Where did that dragon go? Because, he's the one I was hoping to drag into the spring over there and have my way with." She brushed her thumb across his lips, playing with the bottom one. He had such a sensual mouth and she planned to enjoy having it all over her body.

Cage's face finally went from wide-eyed and good guy to bedroom eyes and the dirty dragon she couldn't wait to get to know.

"Oh, he's right here. Ready and waiting for your dining plea-sure." Cage slid his hand over hers and lifted her palm to his lips. He pressed a gentle kiss there and then another to her wrist, nibbling at the sensitive skin above her pulse. "Mmm, I love the flavor of you. I can hardly wait to taste your sweet pussy."

Well, that escalated fast.

"Come on, I'm sure I actually taste a whole lot like dirt and brimstone. Let's go get naked in that water over there."

He laughed and lifted her into his arms again.

"I'm not going to spontaneously burst into my tail again—you don't have to carry me." Shut up, mouth. Azy was secretly loving being picked up and carried by him. The feminist part of her brain said he was being a He-Man and she should show him his place, beside her not above her. The sexual, sensual siren part of her said just because he was being all dominant alpha male, that didn't mean he was a misogynistic asshole. Just a really strong one who also happened to want to get naked.

Girls like Azy didn't get picked up and carried around. Not by any of the men in her human life anyway. The mermen she'd met so far were not the best at wooing. Most of them hadn't wanted anything to do with her.

Screw them all, because she was very happy being carried around and turned on by it.

She wiggled her toes in anticipation as Cage waded into the water. Later, she would take a good long swim around this little spring in her full mermaid form. Right now, she needed legs. So, she could spread them. For him.

As soon as he got in waist deep, she wriggled out of his arms and slid down his body. The water was cool and comfortable, just the right temperature. Cage's skin was scorching under her touch. Azy scooped up handfuls of the water and poured them over his chest, tracing the streams with her fingers all the way down to his belt.

"You're wearing too many clothes. Let's get these off you." She wanted to take her time stripping him. Before she could even say *take off your belt,* Cage was out of his pants and had thrown them over his shoulder.

"Now who is the one with too many clothes on?" He eyed the top of her shirt. "How attached are you to this outfit?"

"They are not even mine. Fallyn gave them to me. I'm not that used to wearing clothes anymore, mermaids don't have extensive wardrobes." In fact, these were the first clothes she'd worn in years.

"Good, then you won't mind if I do this." Cage extended one of his dragon claws and sliced the leather of her shirt right down the middle. He pushed the material over her arms and into the water.

"I have been looking forward to doing this since that dream we had." He cupped her breasts and lowered his mouth to one of her nipples, flicking his tongue across it, before sucking it into his mouth.

Zings of arousal pulsated through her with each lick and suck. They went straight to her center and she wanted her stupid pants off now.

"Cage, I'm still wearing my pants. Let's get rid of them."

"After I'm done worshiping your tits. God, I love how your nipples are just asking me to suck on them, pointing up at me like that."

No man had ever said he even liked her boobs, much less wanted to worship them.

Her ass, yes, her boobs, no. Hourglass, she was not. She had plenty of junk in her trunk, but none of it migrated north. When she used to wear bras as a human, she'd worn a B cup and that was barely.

Guys she'd known wanted a whole lot more.

She'd been self-conscious around the other Mami Wata at first, because it wasn't like they wore coconut bras or seashells. But, at least she wasn't saggy when they were out of the water. Small boobs had their perks. Like being perky.

If he wasn't going to get her out of these damn pants, she would. She pushed Cage away and floated back into the water.

Her own belt still had the mirror he'd given her attached to it. She would ask him about how he'd gotten it later. For now, she carefully pushed it toward the shore, asking the water to keep it safe for her. A small swirling eddy grabbed the mirror and the mirror washed to the water's edge. Another thing to think about later. Perhaps Ky Puru would be able to guide her in this newfound power.

Leather and water did not mix well and Azy had a hard time tugging the leggings off. "Bring that claw of yours back over here."

She'd have Cage slice down the sides of each of her legs. Then the pants would fall off easily.

Cage grabbed her around the waist, flipping her to face away from him and lifted her ass halfway out of the water. "I worship your tits, but I have been having wet dreams about this ass."

The sharp tip of his claw poked between her back and the inside of the back of the pants. In one fast motion he cut through the leather, bearing her bum to the sea and sky. He palmed one of her butt cheeks with his free hand and ran his thumb along the sensitive skin in between.

"I want to take you in every possible way. Will you let me fuck this luscious ass of yours?"

Jesus. Those zings of arousal she'd gotten before were nothing compared to the crashing waves those words sent straight to her clit.

She wasn't ready to admit that she had never been with a man in that way. She was no virgin, but her experiences were slightly limited and were all at least five years old now. No wonder she was so fucking horny all of a sudden.

"We'll see about that. Let's go for the basics this time around, okay?"

"Has anyone ever taken you here before?"

Well, shit. There went that secret. She wasn't going to lie to him, she just hadn't planned on revealing all of her sexual history right away. "No one's ever offered before."

"I'm offering. I'm definitely offering. I promise to make that good for you. We'll get you nice and relaxed after a whole lot of orgasms." He gave her butt one more squeeze and turned her around in his arms again.

Who was she to say no to a whole lot of orgasms? "Sounds great, but nobody's having any orgasms until you get these goddamn pants off me."

"Yes, ma'am." He slashed the pants right off of her, never even touching her skin with his sharp claw.

Finally, there was nothing between him and her except the blessed water. Azy raised one leg and then the other, wrapping them around his waist once more. Only this time instead of a hard belt buckle, she found a hard cock.

"Why aren't you already inside of me?" She maneuvered her hips so that his hard length nestled between her lower lips.

"Fuck, woman. I don't know."

Azy felt like the last two weeks, wearing his shard, and the last few hours running around hell and escaping the Black Dragon, had all been foreplay and she didn't need any more. "Fuck me, Cage. Fuck me right now."

He didn't do as she told him to. Instead he thrust his hands into her hair and brought his mouth down on hers. His tongue thrust into her mouth in the way that she wanted his cock to drive into her pussy. But, oh his kisses were deep and intense, like her mouth was the most important thing in the world to him. He stroked his tongue along hers, tasting her, giving her his spicy flavor in return.

He broke the kiss and stared into her eyes. "Your dirty mouth will get you everything you want from me."

"Apparently not, you're still not fucking me." She wiggled her hips just to remind him about what she was asking for.

His eyes rolled up to the sky and he grabbed her around the

waist, pushing her away. "I'm not going to be able to fuck you if you keep doing that, because I'm going to explode right here right now in the water."

"That can be taken care of with the whole put your cock inside of me thing."

"Babe, if I do that now there won't be any orgasms for you." Cage looked around the spring and headed toward an outcropping of rocks on the other side that were bathed in sunlight.

"I beg to differ. Why don't we find out?"

"What we're going to find out is how many licks it takes me to make you come screaming my name." In another few feet they were at the rocks and he had propped her butt on to a nice wide flat one.

"I don't need you to do that. I am perfectly happy with the normal tab A into slot B kind of sex." Mostly because that was the only kind of sex she had.

"That doesn't sound like near as much fun as what I have planned." Cage sank deeper into the water and threw Azy's knees over his shoulders. He nibbled and licked his way up the inside of her thigh.

She had to admit her girl parts were fluttering at the idea of having his head between her legs. There had to be a first time for everything. That was the story of her life since becoming Mami Wata. First time having a tail, first time swimming in the ocean, first time singing underwater, first time catching her own dinner, first time – "Oh, God."

First time having a tongue in her pussy.

Cage slid his lips and tongue from her channel up to her clit. She'd never felt anything like it. Not even her own fingers had created such a riot of sensations so fast.

He did it again, this time holding her open with his thumbs, giving him more access to her folds. He flicked his tongue across her clit, lashing it in rapid pulses.

Holy moly mother of all things. Why hadn't anyone told her

this felt so damn good? "Oh, Cage. I change my mind. Don't stop doing that. Don't ever stop."

He chuckled, and the vibrations sent whole new spiral of pleasure through her. He lifted his head and she groaned. "Didn't I just say not to stop?"

Was that her voice that was so breathy and needy?

"Your pussy is fucking beautiful, I could stare at it all day." He slid one finger into her wetness and dragged her juices up and down her slit. "Look how wet you already are for me."

He lifted that finger and stuck it into his mouth. "Yum, I have a feeling you're going to be my new favorite dessert. The kind I'm going to want to have several times a day."

He slid his fingers back into her and coated them again, this time pushing two digits inside of her. His head followed. His tongue and fingers had her moaning again in a second. "Cage, yes, yes."

Tab A into slot B could go throw itself off a cliff—Cage's mouth on her was a thousand times better than any sex she'd had with the boys back home.

His tongue worked over her clit and he moved his fingers inside of her so that he was rubbing the tips along the top inside part of her inner channel. Whoa. She wasn't sure, because she didn't have anything else to go on, but the spike of sensation that had her inner muscles clenching were a pretty good indication that he just found her G spot. Who knew it even existed?

"Fuck, fuck, fuck. Right there. Oh my God." She grabbed his hair and made sure he didn't move from that spot. "Oh my God, Cage, yes."

The orgasm he'd been building teetered right on the edge. She lost her breath and forgot how to get it back. Then her body took over and she exploded.

Her legs and stomach muscles convulsed along with the pulsing power of the orgasm. She screamed Cage's name in her mind, but her voice was caught somewhere in the swirls of Nirvana.

Cage's motions slowed, but he didn't stop until the last shiver was pulled from her body.

She was breathing so hard, she was surprised there was any air left in the world. Maybe there wasn't because she was seeing sparkles and black blobs in her vision. She might have died. Death by orgasm.

Cage crawled up over her body and kissed her, giving her a taste of her own flavor. "Worth the wait?"

She whimpered. God, she didn't ever whimper. But, her brain was not quite back in her head yet. It was still floating somewhere out in la la land.

"Good. Because now you're going to get everything you asked for."

Hell yeah.

NEED YOU NOW

Cage hadn't even been inside Azy yet and he was completely fucking enamored with her. She was hot and innocent all at the same time. That was some weird kind of fucking turn on.

The sexual confidence she exuded was beyond sexy and had him ready to burst at the slightest touch. Man, that mouth. God help him, at the same time, he wasn't sure she'd ever had anyone go down on her. She'd already admitted she'd never had anal.

The thought of being the first inside of her sweet juicy ass, well, he'd better not think about it, because he'd come all over her belly.

He'd never thought he had a thing for the virginal types, but Azy was so much more than that. Virgins were shy and didn't know what they wanted or even what went where. She knew exactly what she wanted. That was so fucking hot.

Her eyes were closed, and her chest still heaved from her last orgasm. A fantastic glow had spread across her entire body, a golden sheen that shimmered along with the dragon tattoo across her neck and shoulder.

He'd been too busy licking and sucking and fucking to notice that the dragon's tail swirled down the left side of her chest and wrapped perfectly around her perky little tit.

The mark he'd given her was claiming her body as much as he was. Cage traced the outline, circling the rosy brown skin of her areola, swirling his way to her nipple.

It perked up the second his fingers floated over it. This was why he was into smaller breasted women. So damn sensitive and responsive to his touch.

She was the most beautiful woman he'd ever been with. He couldn't stop touching her. The contrast between his skin and hers spiked his arousal even higher.

His cock was screaming at him to slam inside of her, ride her hard and fast and join her in that state of blissful oblivion. What an asshole that would make him.

No, he'd make this really fucking good for her, making sure she came again and again before he did. That wasn't out of some sort of magnanimous generous lover thing either. No. He wanted Azy to crave him and his touch as much as he needed hers.

Because he was a selfish bastard.

For hundreds of years he didn't even venture to think he would have a true mate, one who owned his soul. He'd never admit to anyone how fucking jealous he'd been of Jakob when Ciara showed up.

Seeing the two of them fall for each other had been enough to drive him into the arms of the succubus who'd stolen his soul.

A soul shard could never be taken. Only given.

Yeah, he'd pretended it was about proving his virility, that coming into his Prime hadn't robbed him of his sex drive like it did a generation of dragons before him.

That was all a big honking lie he'd told himself.

He'd gone looking for someone who lit up his life like Ciara had for Jakob. Wanted so badly for the something extra Portia had been able to give him that no other woman had.

He'd wanted her to be the one so much, that he would have given up that piece of his soul even if she hadn't asked.

How he had ever thought the simple allure of a succubus was anything compared to the way he felt about Azynsa was an absolute joke, and not a funny one.

He certainly wasn't going to admit, was having a hard time even thinking about, that there was even the slightest possibility she wouldn't want him back.

They were certainly mismatched. She was afraid of heights and he longed to be in the sky. She needed the water to live, and he was good being in it only about up to his waist and even at that, he'd prefer it to be in a hot tub. Walking her into the spring had pushed the limits of his comfort zone.

Had the Fates made a mistake? Had the White Witch and the First Dragon chosen her for him, but not him for her?

Could they be so cruel?

Even if they were, Cage would do everything in his power to make Azy his for as long as he could. He would savor every moment with her.

"Love, open your eyes. I want to see you when I fuck you."

She stretched her neck to the side and grinned. Her eyelashes fluttered, and her gorgeous honey-colored eyes looked up at him with satisfaction pouring out of them.

"About damn time," she said. Then she wrapped her legs around the backs of his thighs and her arms around his neck, pulling him in for a kiss.

No, the Fates were wrong if they didn't fully believe this woman was his, and he was hers.

Cage suckled Azy's tongue into his mouth and pushed his hips forward. Her heat called to his cock. He reached between them and positioned himself at her entrance.

"Tell me you want me inside of you, Azy."

"I've been saying that for a while."

He pushed the very tip of his cock into her tight cunt. God, she felt so fucking good already. "Say it, love. Say you want my cock in your pussy."

Her eyes closed again, and she moved her hips, trying to get him to thrust into her. "I do."

"Open your eyes and say the words. I need to hear them."

She sucked in a deep breath and stared up at him. "Fuck me, Cage. I want your cock in my pussy. I want you to fuck me fast and hard. I want you."

Yes.

He thrust all the way into her, his mind on overload from her words and the way her body gripped him.

"Oh, god. Yes. Fuck me, Cage. Fuck me." Azy threw her head back and moaned.

He gripped her hair and brought her face back to him. When she was looking him in the eye again, he withdrew a few centimeters and then pushed back in even deeper.

Her muscles clenched around him each time he thrust in and out of her, making her channel tighter with each second.

"Cage, oh. More. Fuck me harder. I need more."

The sun beat down on his skin, it threw a million sparkles across the water, and even its warmth and beauty were nothing compared to being inside Azy. He picked up his pace, slamming into her, never taking his eyes off of hers.

He never experienced this sort of intensity with any other partner. It was as if they could feel each other, driving them each higher and higher.

"Make me come again, please. I'm so close."

Her words pushed him so damn close to coming himself, he had to grit his teeth to hold back. He propped himself on one arm and reached under her ass with the other, angling her hips up.

Her new position let him sink even deeper inside of her.

She blinked several times and her eyes drifted shut.

"Come for me, love. Give me your eyes, let me see you when you come for me."

He felt her cunt spasm around him and her hips jerked.

"Look at me, Azynsa. I want to see into your soul. I want to know you are mine."

She squeezed her eyes tight and then pulled them open for him, at exactly the moment the orgasm washed over her, took her.

The beauty of her coming for him and only him pushed him into oblivion and he sank deep inside of her, his cock spilling his seed into her for what seemed like eternity.

He sank down, knowing he had to be crushing her under his body. In a second, when he found himself again, he'd move. When he pulled away, she groaned and kept his body held to hers with her arms and legs.

"Not yet. Don't go yet." Her voice was a husky whisper.

"I'm not going anywhere." He dropped his head to her neck and nibbled along her mark.

"Mmm. That feels good."

"Tastes good too. Even better than Jada's donuts."

She giggled. "Why'd you have to go and mention food? Always making me choose between my two appetites."

"So, you have an appetite for me, do you?" he teased, but like wanting to hear her say she wanted him inside of her, he needed to know she needed him.

What a big baby he was being.

Nevertheless, he would make her say it again and again.

"I think you know I do. But, I wouldn't say no to some food right about now."

"I'll have to get up, if you want me to feed you."

"Just one more minute. I like the feel of you on top of me like this, inside me."

Fuck. Yeah.

"Say many more things like that and we'll start this whole thing over again." He waggled his eyebrows at her.

"'That's not a very good threat. What if I want to do it again? Hmm? Did you think of that?"

He would never stop thinking of it. "Yes, love. I promise to fuck you all you want. But, first let's get you fed."

She groaned when he finally pulled out of her and he was sorry to see her close her legs. Immediately she rolled off the rock they were on and splashed into the water. The golden scales of her tail shimmered just under the surface.

He watched her swim a few circles around the rocks before coming back up. She was relaxed and happy. In her element.

"I'll race you back to the shore."

"I don't think my doggy paddle will beat you."

"I'll do the swimming. You fly."

That he could do. He shifted into his dragon, stretching his wings wide before jumping into the air and gliding over the water. Azy zipped along under the surface, her hair unfurling into long curls that wound down her back.

He hadn't realized she even had so much hair. It had been wrapped up in a tight bun of some sort at the base of her neck the entire time.

Cage landed on the ground, letting the water ripple over his talons and waited for her to come out of the water. And waited.

She was there, a meter away searching for something on the sandy bottom. He shifted into human form, ready to wade back into the water and help her. Sunlight glinted off her mirror and when she saw it, she grabbed it, surfacing.

"I meant to give that to you as a gift. I didn't realize it was already yours. Something compelled me to get it from one of my lairs before I left for Africa. Probably the influence of the White Witch."

Azy held the mirror against her chest. "I've had dreams of this mirror since I was little. Some where my mother gazed into it. Some where it was hidden in a dark place. Once with the face of a dragon in it."

She smiled up at him and walked out of the water. The water ran off her naked body in rivulets and he instantly wanted her all over again. "God, you're beautiful."

Her laugh went straight to his cock.

"That's the sex talking. I'm average-looking at best. My boobs are too small, my butts too big, and I can't do a damn thing with my hair when it's drying like this." She set the mirror down and swirled her hair back into the knot it had been in before. "Girls back home hated to get their hair wet. I hate it when mine is dry."

Cage put his hand over hers. "Leave it down. It's beautiful. Your boobs and butt are fucking perfect."

"Wait till you see the other Mami Wata and then tell me what you think." She huffed, but she did let her hair dangle down her back.

"I've only got eyes for you, babe."

She narrowed her eyes at him, but he saw the smile she tried to hide. He would have to tell her a whole lot more how stunning she was to him and work on that reaction.

"Aw, crap. What are we going to do for clothes? I am not meeting the other dragons and their mates naked. It's bad enough Ky Puru has seen me that way and now I have to face him knowing he has."

Cage didn't want to be jealous. Ky had a mate that he was very much in love with, but if he could pluck that particular memory of being in hell with Azy, naked apparently, he would.

"You won't have to. Those were on the shore when I landed." Two piles of clothes. A golden dress with sparkling beads dangling from it and a t-shirt and jeans for him.

"Toga lady?"

"I think so."

She picked up the dress, held it out, and slipped it over her head.

Cage almost ripped it right back off of her. It fit her perfectly, hugging those curves immaculately, yet flowing around her. The way the beads fell and shimmered, it appeared as though she was wearing his scales.

He was buying her an entire wardrobe made out of the exact same material, all in his gold coloring, when they got back to The Lindens. He could take her shopping in Amsterdam or pop over to London or Paris if she wanted. All he knew was that he wanted to see her in, and later out of, that color every day for the rest of his life.

"Why are you looking at me like that. Is this dress too tight? Does it make my butt look big?" Azy turned around and smoothed the material over her ass.

He grabbed her around the waist and joined her in rubbing his hand up and down her plump bum. "It makes you and your butt look amazing. So hot I want to take it back off you and fuck you six ways till Wednesday."

"Oh," she said. "Only six ways? I thought you'd be more creative than that."

Azy walked off in the direction the women had dragged Ninsy, with a definite extra sway in her hips.

It took him a second to quit staring, put his own clothes on and follow her. When he caught up, he slid his hand into hers and walked with her into the camp.

Jakob and Ky were there, looking at some sort of map, and Ciara and Jada were lounging in chairs with fruity umbrella drinks. Ciara pulled her sunglasses down and watched the two of them approach. She threw a piece of pineapple at Jakob.

Jakob turned just in time to catch the fruit in his mouth. He chewed and then said, "Cage. You dumb bastard. We were about to launch a rescue mission to come after you."

Ky slapped him on the back. "Bro, you're a fucktard. But, I see you found your mate."

He smiled over at Azy and gave her a salute. "Azynsa. Good to see you alive and well. Your sisters have been worried."

"Thank you, Ky Puru. I'm anxious to see them."

Jada cleared her throat behind them.

"Right. Sorry we left you down there, *wahine*. Jett assured us you weren't there. Should have known better than to believe a rogue like him."

"Where are Jett and Fallyn?" Azy looked around the campsite.

Ciara came up and handed Azy a drink and a smile. "Ninsy's taken Fallyn to her tent to calm down. She was damn spitting mad. I wanted to help, but she kept yelling weird things at me and throwing daggers at Jakob."

Azy wrapped her arms around herself. "She's had a rough life."

"Ky filled us in. We promised her no dragons would touch her before she let Ninsy take her anywhere. I took her some food. Oh, I bet you're starving too. Come on. I've got a spread in our tent."

The women led Azy away.

"Love, I'll come find you in a few minutes. I want to fill the other Wyverns in on some of what we learned." They needed to be prepared for the Black Dragon's retribution for kidnapping Fallyn. Cage didn't want Azy feeling any guilt over that action. She was right to want to help the woman, even if he didn't fully understand why she'd wanted to.

As soon as she was out of earshot, he turned to Ky and Jakob. "We've got a problem."

SOULFULL

*D*ear God, there was something about these donuts that filled every emptiness in Azy's body and soul. But, only until she was done eating. She'd had a half a dozen of them at least already and she was still hungry. That was what came of only eating scraps for weeks on end and apparently hanging out with a succubus who knew how to bake.

Cage had gone off to talk to some other dragon warriors who had come down to Africa to mount a rescue mission, including Ky Puru, who was definitely not dead.

He'd left her to eat with these women. They had filled her in on both of their matings and how Cage's shard had ended up down in hell without him. They were well beyond introductions now and had moved on to serious girl talk.

Azy hadn't been entirely comfortable with their line of questioning, but Ciara had wrapped an arm around her and suddenly she had opened right up like they were all old friends.

"You only had sex with him once, just this morning?" Ciara blinked at her like that was completely outside the realm of possibilities.

"Yeah. There wasn't exactly a good time or place…in hell."

Ciara shook her head. "I mean, I just can't believe you were able to keep your hands to yourself around him. I wanted to jump Jakob's bones the second I met him. Although, we didn't actually do anything until he marked me."

"Same. I had my tongue down Ky's throat about ten seconds after we met." Jada waggled her eyebrows and bit into another donut. "Then there was that whole period where he pissed me off, and then we had lots of sex."

Ciara nodded. "Oh, right. I think it's obligatory for them to make us mad first. It's like part of the ritual or something. Fleur got so irritated with Steele, that's Jakob's second, that she made him sleep in a cold bathtub."

Jada laughed. "Ky would probably love that. Get him anywhere near water and he turns into a complete horndog. I can't even do dishes at the shop without him trying to get in my pants."

"Tell me about it. Our bedroom is practically its own state park."

"So, their element gets them turned on?" Cage's powers lay in the sun and sky. How was that going to work when she was not only a mermaid but had a newfound ability to ask the water to do what she wanted?

"Yeah. I imagine a gold dragon would make a bed of clouds or something."

Azy had better get over her fear of heights real fast. "Did either of you ever question whether this whole mating thing was real? If your mate was really the right one?"

She wanted to take the words back as soon as they were out of her mouth. What a stupid question. Of course not. Look at how happily in love and lust they both were with their dragons.

Ciara snort laughed. "Oh, god yes."

What?

"Who has ever heard of a super-hot, studly dragon shifter

falling in love with a chubby wedding planner? I certainly hadn't. At least you two knew dragons even existed. I was a plain old human who thought magic was only in the movies until recently."

Jada poured them all more coffee. "I'm pretty sure I tried to talk Ky out of being anywhere near me. Demons don't even mate."

"But, the White Witch is like a Russian babushka when it comes to match making. You gotta do what she says and trust her."

"Who's that?"

"You know, the lady in white who gave you your necklace."

Azy reached for where the shard used to hang around her neck and shook her head. She glanced over to the other women's necks. They both wore shards. One green and one blue.

"You probably didn't realize it was her. I got mine at a flea market. Fleur thought her mother left hers for her." Ciara tapped her lips. "Let me think if I got a vision of yours. Part of my gifts makes me connected to the other mates. What did your necklace look like?"

Despite whatever calming magic Ciara was using, something uncomfortable formed in Azy's throat. Like she'd swallowed too big a bite of donut, and it was lodged just above her esophagus. "I don't have a necklace."

Ciara exchanged a look with Jada that Azy didn't miss for even a second. "Well, um. You probably didn't need one because you already had Cage's soul shard."

"Yeah. That's probably it." Or she wasn't Cage's mate at all.

"So, tell us about the woman Jett brought up? Is she really the one who almost killed Match?" Ciara very adeptly changed the subject.

"Match is the Red Dragon Wyvern?"

The women nodded.

Ninsy, the gold toga wearing woman, had assured Azy that she would take care of Fallyn. That it was her duty.

"I couldn't leave her down there, not after what I saw her father do to her."

"I don't understand how the Black Dragon has a daughter." Jada picked up another donut covered in sprinkles and took a bite. "Or how he's kept her secret for so long. I thought Leon knew everything that went on in the demon world."

Little snowflakes flurried in the air at the top of the tent. Ciara stood and paced back and forth. "Yeah, but he didn't know what Portia was up to either."

That statement seemed to make Jada sad. She flicked the sprinkles off her donut. The snow over Ciara's head melted and raindrops smacked her in the face. She threw her hands up in the air and then wiped them away. "I'm sorry, Jada. I know she is your half-sister. I just feel a little protective over Cage. He was the first dragon who was nice to me."

That was interesting. Had anything gone on between Ciara and Cage?

She was certainly pretty enough. A blonde curvy bombshell much more suited to Cage's movie star good looks.

Ciara turned suddenly and frowned at Azy. "You don't have anything to worry about with Cage and other women. Not that I would ever cheat on Jakob, but even if someone was looking, Cage is head over heels, or rather head over tail, in love with you."

Okay. "I didn't say anything. Are you psychic?"

"No. I have the ability to sense emotions. Your jealousy and worry practically smacked me in the face."

"I hate it when she does that." Jada smiled at her.

"Sorry. I'm still kind of new to the whole white witch thing. Before Jakob kidnapped me, I thought my powers were just because Iw as good at my job. Now, I weather all over people. I'm working on that."

A cool breeze moved through the tent and a swirl of beautiful white light swished into the room and concentrated itself near the doughnuts. Azy blinked and then instead of light, a beautiful woman with long flowing hair almost as dark as hers, olive skin, and a white dress was sitting next to Jada. She picked up a doughnut and a cup of coffee floated into her hand. She dunked the doughnut in her tea as if she had been sitting with them the whole time.

"Well, Jakob was just following his instincts, and it was the fastest way to bring you two together." She took a bite and coffee dribbled down her chin. "Jada, these are divine."

Neither of the other two women said anything, probably because their jaws were on the floor. Not literally but almost.

It wasn't like Azy knew what to say to the apparition, so she waited for the women to get their senses back. Jada recovered first, but instead of saying anything, she topped up the woman in white's cup of coffee.

Ciara finally found her voice. "Mrs. Bohacek?"

"Ciara, dear. I think you can call me Inanna now. Your magic coming along?"

Ciara tipped her head and a little tray with sugar and creamer floated over to Inanna.

"Well done." The woman took three cubes and plopped them into her mug. Then she turned to Jada. "Portia's fine. She's at the seat of the Gold Wyr and giving her mates a helluva time."

"Mates?"

Inanna did not reply to Jade's question and turned her attention to Azy. Her gaze was completely disconcerting as if she knew all of Azy's secrets. They stared at each other for longer than was comfortable, for Azy anyway. Inanna didn't seem bothered in the least. She sipped on her coffee and crossed her legs.

"Do we need to leave?" Jada asked.

Inanna set her coffee cup down and shook her head. "No, it's fine. You won't remember I was here anyway."

"Damn." Jada didn't actually seem to be that bothered by the news.

"I'm going to try to remember," Ciara said.

Inanna again didn't respond. "Azynsa, I owe you a debt of gratitude."

"Why?" She didn't understand who or what this woman was, but she could feel the power emanating from her. All nonhumans had a magical aura and Azy had not understood what she was sensing when she was younger. She didn't understand until her father's death had left a dark place where his aura used to be.

"You get your strong sense of justice from him, little dragon daughter. I am glad he passed that on to you before he was killed."

Azy had a million questions but couldn't get any of them out past the lump the size of Gibraltar in her throat. "How do you know about my father?"

"He is one of my sons, as you are one of my daughters."

This was a confusing conversation that Azy didn't want to have anymore. She looked to Ciara and Jada to help her out, but they were both frozen in time. "I don't understand. I know my father was special, but he was just a cop who was shot by a gang. My mother was a mermaid who left me in his care. Also, I thought there were no such thing as female dragons. How can I be a dragon daughter?"

"We all have secrets, dear. Your father was very special. Kur and I were very sad when he lost his battle to the demon dragons, protecting you."

Rage bubbled up inside of Azy. "My father was killed in a gang shooting. It was my fault. I never should have told him they were harassing me."

She had never said that out loud before. The words burned like acid coming out of her mouth.

"Look inside your heart, Azy. Your mind has protected you

from the truth for long enough." Inanna waved her hand over Azy's face and the tears came.

She let them flow, knowing they were helping to heal old wounds from the inside out. When she was all cried out, Inanna floated a handkerchief across to her. "After you leave, will I remember my father was a Blue Dragon that was slain by Kur-Jara's bastards?"

"Some of that you always knew in your heart."

So, that was a no. That was okay for now, because Inanna had repaid whatever debt of gratitude she felt she had by allowing a part of Azy's soul to heal. "Why did you feel you owe me a debt?"

"You have corrected one of my greatest failings. And I have many. We've been searching for our little Red Dragon for far too long. I knew my sister was involved, but I couldn't risk her knowing I was on to her. Even after everyone else gave up on our girl you did not. For that I will be eternally grateful."

"Fallyn?"

Inanna floated the handkerchief back over to herself and wiped a tear away. "I'd like to leave you with two things. One a token of my thanks and the other a gift for Fallyn. Will you give it to her for me?"

Azy nodded. "But, you don't need to give me a gift."

"Well, then think of it as a gift for Cage. I think he is feeling a little lost because he hasn't followed the same path as his brother Wyverns to find you. This should help."

Azy touched her neck and a necklace appeared in her hand. She lifted it and looked down to see a miniature of her mother's mirror with a shining golden pearl set in the middle. When she looked back up, Inanna was gone.

"What was I saying?" Ciara plopped down next to Jada. "What were we talking about?"

Jada yawned. "I don't know. I'm still not entirely a day person. It's my nap time. And by naptime, I mean sexy times with Ky and then I'm out like a light until around midnight."

Ky Puru stuck his head into the tent. "Did I hear something about a nap, *aroha*?"

Ciara frowned and looked over at Azy. "Azy, I thought you didn't have a necklace?"

She glanced down at her hand and a beautiful miniature mirror with a golden pearl sat in her hand. "Umm, oh. This old thing?"

For some reason she didn't want to talk about how or where she'd gotten it. She did have a strong desire to show it to Cage.

"Thanks for the food, ladies. I'm going to check in on Fallyn. Then I think I could use a nap myself. Hell wasn't exactly a restful place."

She was tired, but after the food and chatting with the other mates she felt lighter, like a dark spot on her soul had been blotted out. Plus, she liked Jada's idea of naptime.

Azy found Cage with Jakob and they were deep in conversation.

"You take her to The Lindens. I'll make sure Match stays in Poland. But, I don't want to keep him in the dark any longer than we have to. If Kur-Jara is going to mount an attack, the Reds should be fighting by our sides."

Cage was going to say something else, but stopped and turned to look over his shoulder, directly at her. She gave him a shy wave.

Wait, why was she feeling shy now? Maybe because she couldn't get all the naughty things they'd done together out of her mind now that he was looking at her with that smolder in his eyes?

Yeah. That was it.

"Agreed. AllWyr at The Lindens then." Cage walked away from Jakob who had a very knowing look in his face.

"Hi. How was your meal?" Cage wrapped his arm around her waist and brushed his lips across hers.

"Good. Interesting. Ciara and Jada are…nice."

"Nice?"

"Yeah."

"Good. I have a feeling Ciara is going to try and talk you into letting her plan a few events for you."

"Really? She didn't say anything. What kind of events."

"The kind with rings."

Rings? Like wedding rings? Azy was not ready to talk about getting married. She promptly changed the subject. "I'd like to go see Fallyn. I have something for her."

Wait, she did?

A white handkerchief was in her hand, and it was wrapped around something hard. She opened the material and revealed a necklace with a sparkling red phoenix charm with a ruby for an eye.

"Pretty. It's definitely shiny so, I'm sure she'll love it. But, can it wait until we get back to my home in the Netherlands? I'd like to get our group back there as soon as possible and get Fallyn under the watchful eye of my guard."

"Uh. Sure. I guess so." She rewrapped the necklace. "You live in the Netherlands?"

"Yeah. I think you'll like it. There are canals everywhere, lots of water for you to splish and splash, since half the country is below sea level."

She was used to warm waters off the coast of Africa. Didn't it snow in the Netherlands? She hadn't seen snow in years. "I don't know of any Mami Wata who live that far north."

"Is that important to you? You can invite them up if you want."

"We'll see." Azy didn't think they'd come. Maybe the three women who had come all the way to Illinois to get her when her father died would. But, the rest of the Mami Wata did not like change.

Azy had lived through some damn big changes in her life and it seemed like another was in order. She would have to make some allowances and sacrifices in her life to adjust to Cage's.

But, wait. When had it become her job to fit into his life?

Maybe he should be trying to fit into hers.

A fish and a bird could fall in love. But, where would they live?

HATE ME TODAY

$\mathcal{C}$age could hardly wait to get Azy back to The Lindens. He needed to know that she would be safe from any demon Dragon attacks. He was very much looking forward to fucking her in a proper bed, underneath the domed skylight in his master suite.

He would revel in her body, give her everything he had.

Once they were back there he could finally feel like they were no longer running from the Black Dragon. A good warrior knew when to retreat to home base. The Lindens was highly defensible, and his warriors were well-trained. Every one of them would be prepared to lay down their lives to protect her and any other mate.

Would any of his golds have mates already?

It was quickly becoming a more and more dangerous world for women fated to love dragon warriors. Ciara, Fleur, Jada, and Azy had all been targeted and attacked by the Black Dragon and his forces. They all needed to be more vigilant and protect their mates.

The sickening taste and burn of bile hit Cage in the back of the throat. He had no doubt that if anything ever happened to Azy, he would not survive.

He couldn't even think about what she'd already been subjected to at the hands of the demon dragons without a dark rage building inside of him.

He was getting her as far away from Africa as possible and assigning half his guard to protect her. First he had to get her home.

"I've got a small private jet coming in to fly you, Ninsy, and Fallyn to my home in the Netherlands."

Azy wrinkled her nose but nodded. They walked together toward Ninsy's tent. She wanted to see Fallyn and he wanted to let Ninsy know of their strategic retreat.

He sped up wanted to get this task out of the way. After they checked in he would feed Azy again and take her to bed. He needed to hold her, connect with her, feel her body around his, to know that she was his and that she was safe.

Both his need and his anxiety for her had grown intense while she'd been chatting and eating with the other women. Several times during his debrief with Jakob and Ky, he'd been ready to leave them to strategize what the new intel, having Fallyn, and Jett's disappearance all meant and how to better fight against the horde.

"I think you'll like The Lindens. It's been in the Wyr for generations. I've been day dreaming about swimming naked with you in the indoor pool."

Azy made a small sound, like a "Hmm."

She was probably nervous about flying again. He would keep her safe. No plane was going down on his watch.

He had a few precious hours before everything would be ready for their departure. Plenty of time to give her a half a dozen orgasms at least, get her nice and relaxed.

Then he could get her to safety. Give her every comfort in the world. After all she'd been through, she deserved it.

"You'll love it, I promise. What you don't love, we'll change. Okay?"

"Sure." She dragged her feet through the dirt.

But first they needed to get off this god-damned continent and as far away from the Black Dragon's caldera as soon as possible.

He would be flying alongside the plane on their trip, ensuring there were no surprise attacks. Demon dragons couldn't take to the skies. But there was no knowing what the Black Dragon could do.

Jett had completely disappeared after the escape from hell, which pissed him off. Cage needed to ask him a few fucking questions about the Black Dragon. It was hard to prepare against an enemy that they had very little intelligence on. He did not like flying into battle blind.

That's all they'd been doing. For years.

All they knew was from his and Ky's experiences in the Black Dragon's realm.

Jakob suggested they try questioning Fallyn.

Ha. Hilarious. They'd gone to see her briefly. She hadn't been afraid of any of them but had told them to be careful because dragon warriors were probably after their souls.

Ninsy didn't let them talk to her for very long. She was as protective of Fallyn as Juliet's nursemaid.

Cage reached for Azy's hand, wanting the way she grounded him, centered him. There was nothing beside him but air.

"What if we don't all go to the Netherlands?" Azy had stopped walking beside him. She stood a meter behind him, staring at the ground, her hands clenching and unclenching in fists.

A sensation like too much coffee on a late night after a bar fight had Cage's heart jumping up and waving a red flag.

"Sweetheart, I know you don't like to fly. But we need to get you and the other women to safety as soon as possible. And that means getting as far away as possible from the caldera and Africa.

I know this oasis has been a level of protection for us, but I don't want to push our luck."

He could practically feel the depths of hell creeping up on them now.

"Azy?" She wouldn't look at him. Why wouldn't she look at him? "Azynsa, what's going on right now?"

He wanted to touch her, feel their bond. For the first time since he had first seen her in all her sword and glory coming to his rescue, there was a wall between them. He didn't think he had put it there. He only wanted to protect her, to keep her safe.

She fingered the mirror she'd hung back on her belt. Not saying anything for a minute or was it an eternity? She was upset, and Cage had no idea why or what he could do to fix it.

If she didn't want to move to the Netherlands, he would adjust. Half of his Wyr would flip their shit, but it was too god-damned cloudy there anyway.

Was that what she wanted? He'd like to take her in his arms and force her to talk to him. Even he wasn't that dumb. The results would be disastrous.

Plus, she'd probably kick his ass.

Finally, she took in a breath and spoke.

"For a long time, I have been in reaction mode. When my father died, I thought I would fall apart. He was my whole world." She looked up at him and tears shimmered in her eyes.

Damn. Their time together had only been about escaping and mating. He swore as soon as they were safe and had a little breathing room, they would spend long days and nights simply talking.

Well, sex and talking.

He reached for her hand, wanting to comfort her. "I'm sorry about your father. I didn't know. I promise I will be there for you through this."

Azy took a step back. "You're not listening. It's not about him. It's about me. When the Mami Wata showed up, I never questioned whether I wanted to change my whole life. I didn't think I had a choice at the time, so I went with them."

Cage wouldn't have felt like he had a choice then either. He understood what it meant to fulfill family and heritage expectations. Sometimes, no, all the time, he did what was right for the Gold Wyr. The Mami Wata had done what was right for Azynsa.

Everyone needed to be taken care of sometimes. That's what family was for. His brother Wyvern's had proven that to him more times than he could count.

A shimmer of light flashed at her neck and spread outward like a layer of protection over her. His own shard responded in kind.

But then the light faded, sinking into the skin at her chest. "Not once did anyone ask me what I wanted."

Well, shit. He certainly hadn't. He never questioned that Azy would be his mate. He had worried they weren't right for each other but had decided all on his own he would make it work between them. What if that's not what she wanted?

He swallowed hard, pushing back the dread in his question, so as to make his delivery flat. He didn't want to influence her response with his own need, as great as it was. "What do you want?"

Azy's face snapped up. The tears were gone, replaced with an emotion he wasn't sure he understood. Surprised that he had asked? Determination to fulfill her own wishes now? Was there anything in there for him?

"I'm not entirely sure. But I know I don't want to leave here. I don't want to run anymore. It's all we have been doing." There was no whine in her voice, no hey-what-about-me. A new defiance rang through.

It was beautiful and scary. He didn't have time for her to question the plan.

"We've been surviving. We had to escape, I had to rescue you."

Uh-oh. He absolutely understood the new look on her face. It was an all-out fuck you.

Those tears from before reflected the anger inside of her. "Maybe I didn't want to be rescued. Do I look like a damsel in distress, dragon?"

Azy was anything but that. "I don't think that for a second."

Cage licked his lips and looked up at the sun. He needed some divine inspiration to help him say the right thing. His gut said to tell her that he was a warrior, that it was his job to protect her. His gut also slapped him for even thinking about that dumbass move. He decided on the truth instead.

"It was killing me."

They stared at each other for a moment. He hadn't said enough for her to get his real meaning. Already his vulnerability with her had him raw. "I could feel your pain as if it was my own. I felt your sadness, your determination, you overwhelm me with your need. I thought it was to get out of there. I understand better now." He stretched his neck, trying to shake off the tightness bunching there. It was no use. He gritted his teeth and bore the pain. "I couldn't sit by and watch hell consume you."

He prayed she would understand and waited for her response, refusing to look away.

She crossed the space between them and placed her hand on his cheek. He leaned into her, wanting much more than this simple connection.

"Cage. I get it. I felt the same about Fallyn. Maybe we were both wrong." There was a slight tremble in her voice that he hated to hear.

He put his hand over hers and looked down into her honey eyes, searching for clues how to soothe her and make this right. If he had a chance at being the mate she needed and deserved, he needed to take himself out of the equation. "What do you want?"

"I don't want to run."

God, how he wanted to pick her up and run with her. It took

all he had in him not to do exactly that. Fly through the sky right now, take her away from all of this. He did his best to push those urges away. "I know. But what do you want?"

She twisted her hand on his face and took Cage's in it. She brought it to her lips kissing his palm in the same way he had done to her.

"I want this to end. The Black Dragon has terrorized too many people's lives. Mine, yours, Fallyn's, the Mami Wata, and your gold dragons." Her eyes flicked back and forth, studying his, assessing. "We need to end it. Let's take the battle to him. What I want is to destroy him."

Ninety percent of Cage's entire life was about being a warrior, fighting the plague of demon dragons without question. He fought for what was right. He never asked for anything in return. That was not the Dragon warrior way.

He brushed off fear like it barely existed, nothing more than dust motes compared to clouds. He knew now that was because he hadn't fully experienced true fear.

This visceral emotion gripped his heart with a fist of razors, shredding him from the inside out. Because he knew he couldn't give Azy what she wanted.

He would never let Kur-Jara lay his eyes on her again.

She would be pissed. She would rail at him, probably threaten him, and fight him for all she was worth.

She would hate him for taking this choice from her.

He would let her. He would hide her from the world. Lock her away in a golden tower. He would bear her hatred like a black mark on his soul, if only it would keep her safe.

He was a coward, and she was his greatest fear.

FEAR AND LOATHING IN AFRICA

*F*ear flashed across Cage's face. The skin at his eyes bunched and he returned a pained stare as his answer. He tried to hide it, but she didn't miss the abject terror her wants and words had caused in him.

He wasn't going to help her destroy the Black Dragon. He wasn't going to listen to what she wanted or even try to give it to her. He was going to take everything from her. Including her heart.

A ping of pain hit her in the back of the jaw and spread across her throat. Nope. No. No way.

She was not going to cry.

There's no crying in love and war.

Cage wasn't prepared to stand with her through thick and thicker.

That hurt like a shard from a broken mirror slicing her open. They were mates, but they weren't meant to be together. Not like this.

She understood. He was going to do what he thought was right, just like her father had, just like she had.

At least Cage and her father had acted out of love.

Maybe, for the first time ever, Azy was too.

Love for herself.

She released his hand from hers and stepped away, lifting her chin.

"You're not going to help me fight Kur-Jara, are you?" She wasn't sure why she asked, she knew. Perhaps, she was just giving him one more chance.

God, she wanted him to take it.

"Azy." He didn't have to say it, the please-understand-I-can't was in his tone. In one word he'd confirmed her greatest fear.

They weren't enough. Together, they weren't strong enough to face what the world had to offer.

She held up her hand, stopping him from saying anything more. Breaking what she'd thought they had even further. "Don't."

He tried to pull her to him, but she pushed him away and marched off toward Fallyn's tent. If this was anything like what Fallyn felt when Azy had insisted she escape hell, gah. Azy deserved to feel the pain of betrayal.

Stupid dragon. Stupid mermaid.

Cage followed, so she stopped, turned and poked him in the chest. "Leave me be for a while. I need to think."

He stared at her for a moment, hulking over her. It would be so easy for him to simply throw her over his shoulder and cart her away. Or transform into his big gold dragon form and whisk her away.

Cage looked away and swore under his breath. "We have a few hours before the plane gets here. You have until then to figure out how stupid you're being. Dragon warriors have been fighting the darkness for millennia. We aren't going to be able to defeat the blackest soul in existence just because you want us to. It will mean the end of us."

He turned and stomped off. She didn't try to stop him. It wouldn't do any good. She'd seen the same behavior in her father growing up. She'd spent many a Friday night at the library instead of at the mall because once he'd made up his mind what was best for her, there was no argument.

Azy was a child then. They'd lived in an area where danger was prevalent and kids like her, black girls from working-class single-parent homes rarely went anywhere in life. Most got into gangs, or got pregnant, or worse. Her father had wanted a better life for her and had been overprotective to help her stay out of trouble.

Azy learned the difference between right and wrong. Injustice and doing good for the world around her. She hated to see anyone bullied or abused. What she hadn't learned was what to do about it.

No one had ever allowed her to before.

No one had needed her to before.

No one could stop her now.

Azy watched Cage walk away from her, turn his back on her and what she wanted.

A pulsating pain rippled through her chest and spread across her back and neck. She laughed at herself for thinking it was her heart breaking.

Never mind. She wouldn't think about that now. It had been her decision to voice what she wanted, and she needed to accept the consequences for that. She was her own woman, mermaid, a fighter.

Even if that meant she had to do it alone, be alone.

She ignored the pain, pushed it deep inside and went to find Ninsy and Fallyn. It might be too late, but she would apologize for trying to make the same kinds of decisions for Fallyn, taking away her choices, just because her gut thought it was right.

Ninsy popped her head outside the tent before Azy even touched it. With a sideways look, Ninsy looked her up and down, pausing at her neck. Azy was being weighed and measured. She didn't care.

"I see you found your inner strength, my lady." Ninsy raised an eyebrow but then smiled at her.

Azy patted her chest, her hair, trying to imagine what Ninsy was seeing. "That's a really weird thing to say."

Ninsy stepped outside and shrugged. "Am I wrong?"

Hmm. She thought about that for a second. Was that what had happened between her and Cage? Did it take a broken heart to find one's inner fortitude? It shouldn't. If she had strength inside of her, it had always been there. Circumstance may have brought it out.

"No, you're not wrong. I didn't know it was there. But, I do now."

Ninsy nodded and opened the tent flap. "Good, you're going to need it."

Fallyn was sitting in one corner of the place on a rug, playing with something in her fingers. Fire.

Tiny flames danced across her fingers. When they went out, she blew out a new blaze and let it dance through her hand again.

"Oops, there goes one more. Poor girl. The dragon warriors got you too. Sad." Fallyn wasn't speaking to either of them. She wasn't even looking at them.

"Ninsy, is she going to be okay?" Could someone recover from more than a hundred years of brainwashing by Ereshkigal and fire whip lashings by the Black Dragon?

Azy was traumatized just from witnesses one such beating Fallyn had taken. She's borne it to save Azy from that fate. Bringing Fallyn out of hell was the only way to repay her for that sacrifice.

Or so she'd thought.

Ninsy folded her arms and watched the flames as intensely as Fallyn. "She's strong inside, like you. Stronger than any of us can even imagine."

"No, no, silly girl. He'll eat you up." Fallyn sighed and pressed two of her fingers together, extinguishing a flame between them.

The way she was talking now wasn't the same as when she'd had those one-sided conversations with the imaginary Izzy. Maybe she'd developed multiple personalities. Azy remembered reading something about how people who were in horrific situations sometimes protected their minds and blocked out the trauma as a defense mechanism.

Azy would do anything she could to help Fallyn recover. That included avenging the atrocities done to her by destroying the Black Dragon and all who worked with him.

"I have something for her. Do you think it's okay to give it to her?"

Ninsy nodded. "She's been waiting for it."

Now Ninsy was starting to say weird things. Azy went over and knelt in front of Fallyn. She pulled the little package out of the pocket on her dress and unwrapped the necklace.

"Fallyn, my friend. I have something for you."

Fallyn tipped her head to the side and then glanced down at the necklace in Azy's hand. The red gem in the phoenix's eye lit up and the light was reflected in Fallyn's eyes. A literal fire lit in her big black pupils, matching the color of the jewel.

"Don't touch my stuff." Fallyn snatched the necklace from Azy and held it to her chest. "Where are the rest of my shiny things. Give me back my ornaments and daggers. Their mine."

Someday when she was a little better, and the threat of the Black Dragon had been eliminated, Azy would take Fallyn to Chicago at Christmas. They'd go see all the lights on the Mag Mile, the giant sparkling trees, and Azy would buy her all the ornaments she wanted. "I don't have them. But, I promise we'll get you more. Okay?"

Fallyn narrowed her eyes. "Izzy says to trust you. I'm not so sure." She jerked her head to the side, as if she heard something. "Oh, not her too. That dragon will burn her alive with his light. Stupid girl."

"Who are you talking about?"

Fallyn shook her head and sighed again. "No one now. She's gone, like so many others today. That's your fault."

Yeah. A lot of things were on Azy's shoulders now. "What's my fault?"

"You found the Gold Wyvern. Now the warriors are finding all the golden girls in my head. They're eating them up. That's your fault."

Oh. Umm. What did that mean? Didn't matter right now. She just wanted Fallyn to know everything was going to be okay. "I'm...sorry?"

Fallyn shrugged. "The blue and green ones are getting eaten too, but I can protect the red ones. Hide them."

Ninsy put a hand on Azy's shoulder. "You have to go now. Fallyn and I are leaving, I'm taking her back to the land of her birth. But someone has come looking for you."

Uh-oh. Had the Black Dragon found her already? No. The magic in this place hid them all like Fallyn's red people in her head.

Azy popped back out of the tent and looked over the water of the spring. She squinted—the sun's reflection on the water had her seeing mirages. She cupped her hand over her eyes and felt a pile of rocks sink into the pit of her stomach.

Three very tall men, who looked a lot like wet Vikings, walked out of the water and straight toward her.

Shit, shit, shit.

She didn't recognize these men in particular but knew exactly what they were.

Mermen.

What she didn't understand was why they were here. She so did not need these guys in her life right now. Mermen were domineering, testosterone-filled bags of misogyny and racism. The Mami Wata only interacted with them a few times a year. For mating.

Sex only, not true mating.

Not like what she thought she had with Cage.

But what did she know?

Merman believed that magical races should not mix. Which had a lot to do with why they hated her.

Azy stood a little bit taller, trying her best not to show that they intimidated her at all. "Gentlemen."

The tall one in the middle looked her up and down, frowned at her hips, and then dipped his head in greeting. "Azynsa."

Uh-oh. They knew her name. That wasn't a good sign. She sure hoped they weren't here to make trouble with the dragons. They were as powerful as the dragon warriors, but they didn't fight the same kinds of battles.

The mermen were working to conquer new waters. Not all mermaids around the world bowed to their need to be in charge. The Mami Wata had been aligned with the mermen long before Azy came along. She didn't like it but had been instructed to treat them with deference. It was the best way to keep them from bothering her.

"What can I do for you?"

The merman scoffed at her like her question was idiotic. "We are here to take you back to your people. Your time with the dragons is through."

She would have thought they would be glad she was out of the ocean. Regardless, she was not ready to bow to them and be dragged away. She had plans that would do more for the Mami Wata then these dickheads had ever done. "I'm sorry you have wasted your time."

The leader of the pack glared at her. "Your sisters are worried about you. Many fear you are dead. It is our duty to protect them and you."

Cage's voice came from behind her. "You should've thought of that when the demon dragons were attacking them and kidnapped her."

Uh-oh. Azy smelled a pissing match coming on.

Cage in all his golden glory, came up and stood next to her, legs spread wide and arms crossed. The mermen might have been able to take him on, but Jakob and Ky joined in the fun and games.

"Hello there, douchebags of the sea. Caught any crabs lately?" Ky's greeting was not exactly friendly.

Jakob simply growled at them.

"We appreciate your assistance in helping our women in their battle and in rebuilding their home. Your water dragons have been dismissed. We are here now."

"Ta, bro. But I think we will stick around." Seems like Ky had had dealings with the mermen before.

There had to be more to the mermen showing up here and now than wanting her back. She took a close look at the group standing in front of her and noticed they all had burns. They were mostly healed, but she knew what that looked like. They were the burns of a fire whip. They had been battling demon dragons and maybe even the Black Dragon himself.

They weren't here for her, but to ask for the help of the dragons. So, what was up with the façade?

Merman asshole number one stepped toward her, making to grab her arm. Cage stepped in front of her, his scales shimmering across his arms and shoulders.

Ninsy had said she would need her inner strength. Azy felt it bubbling up inside. Or, maybe that was her complete and utter irritation with the males of every species she knew.

She raised her hands into the air, closed her eyes, and very kindly asked the water element to douse them all. It so nicely complied.

The water from the spring swirled up into the air and a handful smacked each of them in the face.

"You can all put your dicks away now. I don't have to do what any of you say, nor do I need anyone's protection from the other. Got that?"

The two mermen who were behind the leader exchanged glances and one of them might've even smiled a little. Interesting.

Cage put his arm around her and said, "Sorry, mate."

Azy picked his fingers up and dropped them into the air away from her, not acknowledging his claim on her.

"Now, shall we all try this again?" About half of them nodded. Azy would take it.

She had an opportunity here and would need all of her inner strength to grasp it, use it for all it was worth. Because doing so meant leaving Cage and what he wanted for her behind.

"Now, why are you really here?"

The smiling merman stepped forward and indicated with a glance that the other merman dickhead should step down. "Demon dragons are attacking all over our realm. Many women have been lost to them. Some of our leaders," he glanced at the douche bag merman, "do not think we need help. They are wrong."

"Good. That's a good start. Now, let's talk about an alliance between the mermen and the dragons. Because together I think we can defeat Kur-Jara."

Cage grabbed her arm and pulled her away from the rest of the group.

"Azynsa, you cannot endanger yourself like this. I will not allow it."

Words she dreaded she would hear from him. She wanted so much for the spark of love between them to be enough for him to trust in her. But it wasn't.

"My actions are not for you to allow or not. If you don't want to be a part of the solution, then go back to your golden castle and protect your way of life. Not mine."

"Azy. Don't do this. Come with me. Let me keep you safe. We'll find another way to defend against the Black Dragon."

"No. I'm going with the mermen to fight."

Yeah.

Cage sighed and bowed his head. "I'm sorry, my love. I truly am."

The hairs on the back of Azy's arms and neck stood on end and her skin tightened.

Those gold scales shimmered over Cage's body again and in a flash, he shifted into his dragon form and snatched Azy in his claws. He jumped into the air and flew straight up toward the sun and clouds.

God damned dragon was kidnapping her.

She beat against his talons until they were too far up into the sky for her to survive a fall. The cold air took her breath away and made her shiver.

Yes, it was the cold air. Not the fact that Cage had truly broken her heart this time.

EVEN DUMB DRAGONS DESERVE LOVE

The anger rolled off his mate in waves, pushing him to fly faster than he ever had. Cage stuck to the warmer currents and pulled upon his power of the sun to keep her warm at their altitude. He felt her shiver anyway.

They moved from her body to his, shaking his core so much he had to concentrate to fly. His wings felt disconnected from him, his shard didn't shine like before.

The skies were clear, which was good because he needed the space and time to clear his head. He'd sworn that he could bear the brunt of her utter rejection of him like a warrior. He'd been wrong about how dark and lonely he already felt without the light of her love.

He thought he could show her that he was everything she needed. He wanted her to crave him.

Then he'd gone and fucked that all up.

They may be fated mates, but they still had free will. If Azy chose not to be with him, decided she wasn't in love with him, even a little bit, that was her choice.

He couldn't blame her for closing herself off from him. Cage had betrayed her so deeply. He wasn't even sure he could forgive himself.

His punishment had already begun. Every fear he'd had about not finding a mate before he'd known about her came rushing back, double fold.

He would never know the joys of love. Not like Jakob or Ky. He would turn into a bitter old man, like Match was already. He'd never know the love of children or true family. He would not have an heir. Because, without Azy, without her love, none of it mattered.

There would be no one else for either of them. That was exactly the way Cage wanted it. It made his heart ache, literally radiate with pain that she would be unhappy, not have any of those things he's wanted for them. But, he could not, would not stand for her to have any other man in her life.

He would live in misery as long as she was safe.

They both would.

He didn't try talking to her during the flight. He doubted she would listen or respond anyway. It would be almost better if she would rail at him. Let him know exactly how much of a lying unbelievable bastard he was.

At least that would be some emotion from her. He wanted to see her mad, just so he could have the tiniest taste of her passion, even if it was bitter.

Being the king of the wind had some advantages. It wouldn't take as long to fly home as it had to get to Africa in the little plane. No rocket-fueled man-made machine could catch him.

He almost wished they could float up here in the sky together forever. Up here, she was in his care, in his arms. She wouldn't let him touch her ever again once they landed.

All too soon the canals and rivers of his homeland came into view. It didn't seem as beautiful as he remembered. No flowers were in bloom, the grass was yellowed, not green, and even the trees drooped. Or maybe that was his view of it now.

He hoped someday she would learn to appreciate the waters around The Lindens. If not, he would build her pools, and springs, and fountains. He would build her a whole damn aquarium and fill it with every creature in the sea, just for her.

Once he knew nothing from hell was coming for her, he would even send some of his warriors to find her sister mermaids and bring any that would come to her. No mermen, however, would ever be invited to his estate. Mermen could all go to hell, and without Azynsa.

If they hadn't shown up he might have been able to convince her to leave the oasis and her plans to defeat the Black Dragon behind. While she'd been talking to Ninsy and Fallyn, he'd plotted and planned to tell her they were going to regroup only. That once they weren't in imminent danger she could have access to all his warriors, his covert ops team, his fortune to hire an army if she wanted.

He wouldn't let her anywhere near a battle.

At least he hadn't had to lie to her.

In another few minutes The Lindens came into sight. His home was not the peaceful place he'd left it. The ground was black with burns and ash. The waters filled with blood. The seat of the Gold Wyr, a stronghold that had been the respite of dragon warriors for hundreds of years was gone.

The muscles that controlled his wings froze, lost the ability to fly, and they dropped hundreds of feet. The sky went dark, or maybe that was just his vision.

First Dragon above, what had happened here?

Azy screamed and clung to him, bringing him back to his senses. He cupped her tight, his talons secured around her, and they glided toward the ground.

He circled the grounds and took in the carnage below. The main house had been razed to the ground. Only a few burnt timbers and glass remained. Great scorches scarred the earth and the bodies of several gold dragons lay strewn around his home.

They'd given their lives, serving and protecting the Gold Wyr.

The battle was over and so was his and all the Gold's way of life. If hell had found this place, even with his ancient wards, and destroyed everything in sight, nowhere was safe.

For the first time since he'd grabbed her, Azy spoke. "Oh my God. Cage, oh my God."

No. God couldn't help them now.

He circled once more, searching, hoping, praying for survivors. Azy spotted them first. She pointed to a band of his warriors on the far side of the training field. Some were in human form, but most were still dragons, which showed how grievous their injuries were if the needed their magical form to heal them.

One man raised his arm. Gris, his second, waved them in, indicating that it was safe to land. He would be able to tell Cage every detail of the battle. Good. That would fuel his rage.

Cage carefully set Azy next to Gris and shifted into his human form. He grasped his second on the arm. They didn't bother to exchange any niceties. "What happened?"

Gris was covered in burns and the ground all around the surviving warriors was littered with black stains, the indication of so many demon dragon deaths, the ground was barely visible beneath the layer of ash.

"A horde like I have never seen. They came out in the middle of the day." Gris shook his head. "I've never seen them in full sunshine like that. They were... bigger, stronger."

Like the ones Jett had spoken to in hell. Cage would hunt that bastard down and favor or no, Jett would help them take revenge on his little buddies. "The Black Dragon?"

Gris nodded. "If that's who he was. He's burst up out of the ground like it was soft clouds, taking us by surprise. He killed the warriors guarding the house before we even knew what was happening. I'm sorry we failed you, my lord."

Cage had felt his home would be safe. How wrong he had

been. How arrogant to think that he alone could protect anyone just because he was a Wyvern.

"No, AmberGris. You are not the one who has failed the Wyr. I have no doubt without you the devastation would have been greater. How many golds are lost?" How many more would be lost in this war?

That's what this was. Before today his life had been a series of battles. He and all dragon warriors had played at games. Now when the real deal showed up, they were unprepared. Cage was the failure. He'd let his Wyr be destroyed because of his own arrogance.

He had let that happen.

No more. If war was what the Black Dragon wanted, it was what he would get. Cage would personally destroy him. He didn't yet know how, but he would kill the Black Dragon and avenge the deaths of his comrades.

Gris looked down at the ground, his hands were shaking. "Three that we know of. But more are unaccounted for. Captured."

"Zon?"

Gris took several deep breaths before he could speak again. "And Portia."

Cage had wondered if she had escaped. "Why would Kur-Jara want the succubus now?"

"There's more. The succubus Geshtianna is working with the Black Dragon. She and her coven. They were here and worked against us." Gris wavered and Cage grabbed him to keep him upright. The man needed to shift and heal.

Holy shit. "We knew Portia had ties to them. Did she betray us?" Again Cage's arrogance came up to bite him in the ass. He hadn't thought Portia was a threat. He thought he could use her.

"No. Never." There was more force in Gris's voice than Cage expected. "She fought by our sides. She was taken because she was defending Zon."

"Are you sure? How else would the black Dragon and the coven –"

Gris slashed his hand through the air. "I'm sure."

Cage had been fleeced by Portia before. While he trusted Gris and his judgment, the succubus allure could mess with a dragon's head. Especially when they were looking for a mate.

"I know because she is my mate. Our mate."

Cage glanced at Gris's neck. He no longer wore his soul shard. "Zon too?"

Gris gave a curt nod. "Yes, she lit up our shards like fucking fireworks."

Cage understood. He glanced over at Azy, who was helping another warrior bandage his wounds. Water flowed through her fingertips, soothing the burns.

"Just like your shard is doing now."

Cage didn't even need to glance down. He felt the tingling buzz of the talisman against his skin. It compelled him to go to her.

Azy looked up from her work and met his eyes. A necklace dangled from a cord around her neck. It glowed with a golden hue too. Cage's gut clenched.

It shouldn't be there. The only thing she should have on was his shard. She'd saved him the first time she wore it.

He would ask her to save him again now.

He clapped Gris on the shoulder and made him a promise. This time, he would use all his resources to keep it. He would not fail his Wyr again. "We will get Zon and your mate back. I swear to you. This is war and with our mates by our sides, we will win it."

The abject grief on Gris's face told Cage he didn't believe it yet. He would.

"Gather the men we have left. We will regroup in Poland at the Red Wyr seat. My mate has a plan to take the Black Dragon down, and we will need every warrior we can find."

He left Gris and went to Azynsa. He nodded to the warrior she was helping and pulled her away.

She yanked away from him, not welcoming his touch. She might not ever again, even after he begged for her forgiveness. He believed with all of his soul that even if they could never be together again, she would use her passion, skills, and inner fire to help him bring down the Black Dragon.

"Is this enough to convince you that we need to fight against this dark evil?" She motioned around to the death and destruction, but Cage saw none of it.

"No," he kneeled to the ground in front of her, "you convinced me. I was just too scared to admit it."

Azy opened her mouth to say something but then closed it again. She sucked in a breath as if she'd found her words but again said nothing.

Cage had never seen her speechless. He didn't really like it either. She was smart and hilarious and would probably save them all.

Oh, what he wouldn't do to see her smile at him again. What he should have done in the first place. Take his own damn needs out and replace them with what he'd known all along was right.

"I am truly sorry for my failing you when you needed me the most. Not in hell, but when you wanted me to believe in you. I realize it may take a long time for you to forgive me. But, I hope you will –"

Azy put her fingers over his lips. "Shut up, dragon. You are a royal dumbass. But for some reason that I don't think has anything to do with being your mate, I am in love with you. And, I learned recently not to harbor or hold grudges against those I love. It's like poison we think we are giving to others but taking ourselves."

Thank the First Dragon. The relief of her words and forgiveness blew across his skin and into his soul like a gentle spring breeze. Nothing in the world could feel better.

Cage stood and grabbed her up in his arms. He kissed her for a good long time, putting all his passion, love, and belief in her into it. He tasted and teased her, ate at her lips, and sucked her tongue into his mouth, until several dragon warriors behind them cleared their throats.

He broke the kiss and pressed his forehead to hers. "I think they are ready to hear your plans to exact some revenge on Kur-Jara."

"You think so, huh?" Her grin lit up his world.

Before another moment passed he would have her and everyone present know how he felt about her. He lifted the soul shard over his head and placed it around her neck. He grabbed the necklace to move it aside and it disintegrated into a riot of colorful dragon scales that swirled and blew away in the wind.

Gold sparkles lit up the air around them and in them he saw a vision of lifelong love, with her.

"Azynsa, my mate, my love. Take my soul. It is safe only in your keeping. I give it to you freely because I love you and know that it belongs to you. It has for a long time."

She placed her hand over her heart. Her bottom lip trembled, and her eyes glistened with tears. "I'll take it," she whispered. "Because I told you back in hell, it was mine."

Cage chuckled. "Yes, you did."

"Don't forget this time." She brushed a soft kiss across his lips. "Because together we are better. We are stronger, and love is going to conquer all."

HELL FREEZES OVER

*W*as Azy still a little bit mad at Cage for basically kidnapping her? Yes.

Was she going to let that stop her from getting her own God damned happy ever after?

Not a chance in hell.

And hell's chances were looking pretty fucking slim at the moment.

She promised herself that when this battle with the Black Dragon was over, they would have that nice long talk about being and alphahole mate with misogynistic tendencies. But, she also planned to have that discussion in bed, while she rode him, cowgirl style.

She could hardly wait, but wait, she would.

They were going to war.

Cage might be a dumbass when it came to love and feelings, but he was a master warrior. His gold dragons were already mobilized and, on their way to recruit the other Wyrs to their cause. He would lead them gloriously into battle and she would be right there by his side.

She and Cage flew to Poland, which was just a hop, skip, and a twenty-minute flight away. Match, the Red Dragon Wyvern was not there, which had his Wyr in an uproar. No one had heard from him, Ninsy, or Fallyn. Cage assured her that Ninsy would protect Fallyn and that after the battle they would all find her.

She had to accept that for now. But, it would be her next priority to find Fallyn again and continue to help her heal.

Gold and Red dragons from all over the area joined them and were preparing for battle now. A battle she'd planned.

Azy had laid out the basics of her idea to Cage and Gris, and the Red second, Brand.

She was no strategist, but she had taken science in school and had gotten an A-plus on her volcano project.

This plan took the volcano and flipped it on its head and inside out. Quite literally.

They were going to destroy the Black Dragon's stronghold. Hell would be no more. Not this little corner of it anyway.

If they were lucky, they would capture or even better kill Kur-Jara and the Black Witch.

Azy was so ready to end this thing.

They would need the power of all four elements to make it work. It was every man on deck, plus every mer down below.

Jakob and Ky were still in Africa and were gathering the troops at the oasis. Cage and his gold flyers were shuttling as many greens and reds to the continent as they could. All, except Gris. Cage had sent him on a special assignment to infiltrate Geshtianna's coven. They did not need any outside forces helping Kur-Jara escape.

Everything was being kept super hush-hush so that they could have the element of surprise. Only the Wyverns, Brand, and the leader of the Mer contingent knew the plan.

She and Cage sent a dozen Red Dragons down to join the battle using the mirror and sword. Azy used the spring as the reflection to send them through. Which the reds didn't like, but they had a particular rage directed at demon dragons and they would be integral in making sure none escaped into the hot lava below, so they grinned and nodded when she said she could get them there faster.

Now, she and Cage were jetting their way down from Poland. Wind whipped across her face and the scent of the sea sprayed through the air. Azy was actually starting to feel comfortable flying. As long as Cage was the one whose leg she could hug like a tree trunk. It helped that he flew low over the water.

"Ready, love?"

The ocean called to her like a long-lost friend. "As I will ever be."

"Okay then. I'll see you back at the oasis, hopefully with the Black Dragon's head on a stick." He released her, and she dove into the water.

She didn't even have to think about her shift—her tail happily appeared.

Azy swam like a mad woman down toward the caves along the coast where she and the Mami Wata lived. Two blue dragons swooped up beside her and she rode in the wake between them, going faster than she would be able to on her own. When they approached the underwater caves, the dragons broke off and were greeted by two of her sister mermaids. Both of them wore blue soul shards.

Azynsa touched the shard on her own neck. She doubted these two would be the last to become mates to dragons. That was probably going to piss a lot of mermen off.

It was time they got over themselves, anyway.

A circle of Mami Wata had formed just outside the entrance to their caves. Several, who she counted as friends greeted her with full on arm to elbow motions flipping her the bird.

She couldn't help but smile. Azy had done her fair share of telling the fish in the sea to fuck off and given them the finger when she had first come to the Mami Wata. Those first weeks after her father was killed and she had to adapt to a very different and new life had been difficult. Many had shunned her at first and did not understand her strange behavior.

Not all Mami Wata had been overly influenced by the pure blood line of crap the mermen had given them and eventually she'd made friends. She had explained to them that her hand signals and swearing was a war cry of her father's people.

That they understood. The Mami Wata had not always been a peaceful race. Azy was planning on tapping into their history of war today.

She returned their greeting with a double-fisted fuck you too. They loved it.

"Azynsa, we are overwhelmed with joy to see you alive and well." A few of the mermaids hugged her. "The dragons say you have become a warrior like them."

She guessed she had. "Yes, and I hope to turn many of you into warriors this day too."

One particularly beautiful mermaid with a green tail swam over and flipped her off. "I don't understand how you have done it, but there are mermen here who are behaving very differently. Most have not made any demands, and some have said things like they are sorry."

Several of her sisters nodded and one said, "What does sorry mean?"

Well, well, well. You can teach an old mer new tricks. She had hopes for her sisters to find good mermen after all. They were equally as hot as the Mami Wata were beautiful. Sex symbols of the sea.

Azy would like to see her sisters happy. And well loved.

"It means they're going to quit being such," she wanted to call them douchecanoes, but that wouldn't translate, "mean men."

"Oh." Several girls nodded their heads, but Azy clearly saw that they did not understand. Maybe after the battle she would help them understand women's lib. She sort of wished Mami Wata wore bras, so they could burn them.

On to business. "Do you all understand what is going to happen and what you need to do?"

The green-tailed mermaid picked up a rock from the ocean floor and smacked it into her hand. "We're going to kill demon dragons, like you."

Okay then. She hadn't actually killed anything besides fish in her life, but if some of the Mami Wata had a blood lust going on, she was going to harness that.

"Good. Be careful. A great many of them will die in the flooding of hell, but those that escape will be dangerous."

"Don't you worry about them—we'll take care of the killing." A group of particularly brawny mermen with wicked looking spears swam up to their group.

Three of them nodded and gave her a little salute. But the one who'd had his hate on for her at the oasis was practicing his glare again.

This should be fun.

The two water dragons circled their group and one approached Azy. *"Ky is on his way down. He says they're ready at the surface, little general."*

Little general. Cute. Better than little mermaid.

"Let's do this."

As soon as Ky joined her, they swam into the caves, asking the sea to swell and join them. Phase one of operation Hell Freezes Over had begun.

She and Ky flooded the underwater caves and made their way into the caverns and tunnels at the base of the caldera, watching for Kur-Jara and his lackies everywhere. They pushed the water across the hellfires and Ky and his blue dragons froze it all making the heat benign.

"You're one smart cookie, Azza. Cage is lucky to have you by his side."

"Thanks, Ky Puru."

"I think you can just call me Ky now."

"No. I don't think so. Sounds too weird."

Ky laughed in her head. Then he swooped forward and speared the first group of demon dragons they encountered with his ice shards.

Yaass. The Black Dragon couldn't be far now. A zip of adrenaline hit her system and she burst through the water at top speed. The shard at her neck warmed and buzzed. She couldn't see him, but she knew Cage was soaring through the air above them somewhere.

A group of mermen behind her sounded a war cry and swam past. The douchie one bumping her along the way.

Whatever, dude.

The dragons and mers divided and conquered the hordes they came across. Azy sent one careening against a rock and watched as it burst into nothing but a black stain.

There weren't all that many and the battle was over quickly. She led the group deeper into the caldera's maze. They would reach the main cavern soon. If they hadn't come across the Black Dragon trying to escape via the water routes, he would either be climbing out toward the sky, where Cage would eat his face off, or retreating to the last part of hell to flood.

When they did, Azy had a little mission of her own.

"Jakob and his greens are ready for phase two, gang. Hold on to your butts." Ky's warning rang out through everyone's heads. The walls around them rumbled and rocks and debris began to fall in great chunks.

Azy took a deep breath, closed her eyes, and concentrated on the spirit of the water element. She felt its power swish and sparkle around her. "There you are, old friend. Help me keep our justice fighters safe from the chaos around us."

As if it was replying, a bubble of lava jumped up under Azy, and the water pushed the danger away, creating a sculpture of newly formed volcanic rock underneath her.

"Thank you."

The ceiling above her opened and she filled the newly created cavern with more water. Still there was no sign of the Black Dragon. Dammit.

Just ahead she recognized the dark room where Kur-Jara had whipped Fallyn and Ky. They were deep underground now, but the earth above them cracked open and rays of intense sunshine lit up the darkness, executing the final step in their plan. Let there be light.

"Hello, love. Having fun yet?" Cage swooped down into the crack in the earth and ran his wingtips along the surface of the water.

Azy poked her head up above the surface of the churning waves she and the element had created around them.

"Not yet. The Black Dragon hasn't been found. But, I have plans to have a lot of fun with you later to make up for that."

"Promise?"

She waved him off and dove back down into the water. If the Black Dragon wasn't here, she was heading for one tunnel and one sparkling cave in particular.

"Be careful."

His words didn't feel oppressive this time. She knew he was genuinely worried about her and at the same time, giving her room to fly, or swim as the case may be.

She swooped through the tunnels until she found the cave she was looking for. The water held everything in the room in suspended animation for her. Not a sword or Christmas ornament was out of place.

Azy opened the bag she'd dragged along and began placing some of the treasures inside. She'd taken away Fallyn's right to choose her life. The least she could do was provide her with what little comforts she'd had down here.

She wouldn't be able to get them all, but a handful were better than none. The last one she grabbed was the mirrored one Fallyn had gifted her to find Cage. She reached for it, but it shattered in front of her eyes. Hit by a spear.

"The water may have protected you once, dragon's whore. I won't miss again."

Azy spun and was not so surprised to see douchie dude blocking the exit to the cave. She moved to swim past him and he blocked her way.

"For fuck's sake. What is your problem?"

"You are." He advanced on her, his spear held at the ready.

She'd seen other mers use their weapons. They didn't miss and the tips were sharp and very deadly.

Great. "Get the fuck out of here."

He laughed at her. "I'll leave soon enough. But, you won't. I can't allow you to continue your muddying of our waters. Most will be happy to be rid of you, and those that aren't will believe that you died cowering in fear from the demon dragons."

If he believed that, he didn't know her or her friends very well. Cage would be the last to take this dickhead's word.

"We're not here to fight each other. Don't you see this is a new opportunity for the Mers and the Mami Wata to work together?"

He swam a circle around her, looking her up one side and down the other. Was he checking her out? Disgusting.

"We don't need to work together. The Mers will always rule over the Mami Wata. We need you only for breeding."

If she didn't think it would make him more volatile, she's slap him. That wouldn't get her out of the cave. It would feel damn good though.

"Look, we can have a nice long dressing down about your misogyny later. We've got Kur-Jara to worry about. He could be here anywhere."

Not likely, but maybe the threat of the big bad Black Dragon would distract him long enough for Azy to figure out a way out of here. A way that involved swords.

"Oh, he's long gone. You don't think we'd let our greatest ally—"

Azy didn't let him finish that sentence. She grabbed one of Fallyn's shiny sharp swords and shot it through the water at his head. "You have betrayed your own people."

"You're the one who has betrayed your people. You have become the whore of a dragon."

"Are you fucking kidding me with this right now? Who died and made you the king? Oh, that's right—nobody. You're just a scumbag who doesn't know his ass from his face."

Okay. That pissed him off.

He exploded across the water and grabbed her by the throat and hair.

"You're an abomination. But, we don't punish the child. Only the sinner. Your mother paid the price. Don't make me kill you too."

This merman was a total bag of dicks.

"You, you, you killed my mother because she had me?"

"She sullied the bloodline. We can't allow that to happen again."

The rock above them opened and some big ass sharp talons grabbed the merman by the shoulders and slammed him into the newly formed side of the crevasse.

"Sorry, babe. Just wanted to help. I'll hold him down for you and you kick his ass."

Cage hovered an inch over the water and held the merman against the stone wall with a talon through his shoulder.

"How did you know?"

"We're connected. Always. Now show this asshole who's boss, huh?"

Adorable. No one had ever held someone down for her to beat up before. Offered to beat an asshole up for her, sure. But, hold him down while she did it herself? How sweet.

Azy propelled herself up through the water and into the air.

She popped up just far enough to kiss her dragon on the cheek before she dove back down into the water.

The water sloshed and swirled around her and she used its energy to pick up Fallyn's collection of swords and aimed them all at the merman.

"Go ahead. Kill me. There are plenty more who feel like I do, and we will never let you and your kind—"

"Shut up, you piece of shit." Azy aimed one very long, thin dagger straight at the merman's dick and shot it through the water, chopping his appendage right off. He screamed and passed out.

"Ooh. That's gonna leave a mark."

"Take him to the oasis. He's been working with Kur-Jara, warned him we were coming. We can probably learn more from him about where he and Erishkigal have gone."

Another gold dragon swooped down and grabbed the merman, or mer-eunuch, taking him away.

"Can I give you a ride, my lady?"

The water and earth swirled around her in a giant muddy crater. Jakob and his greens had opened the earth up, inverting the volcano. The blues had flooded it with water, while the golds had filled the darkness with their light. The reds had dived deep into the earth via the lava to ensure no demon dragons were left in hell.

It was hell no more.

Kur-Jara and Erishkigal had escaped, but together she and Cage had tipped the balance of power out of his favor.

"Yes, please. Let's go home."

SKY HIGH

Cage and Azy lounged on the beach near Malaga. He soaked up the rays and she splashed in the warm water. Perfection.

They were having a new Gold Wyr stronghold built nearby. A lot of Golds had made the move to Spain with him.

There was more sun here and they all reveled in it.

"Why didn't I move down here years ago?"

She splashed water on him with a flick of her tail. "Cause, you're a dumbass dragon who was set in his ways. You needed a woman to come in and set you straight."

"Oh. Right." He laughed. He'd laughed more in the past few weeks than he had in the rest of his life, and he was a pretty fun and games guy most of the time. So that was saying a lot.

He got up out of his lounge chair and headed toward her, already hard and thinking of all the very dirty ways he was going to fuck her and even more ways he was going to make her come. "Who was this brilliant woman?"

She quirked a finger at him. "Come here and I'll show you."

Ciara and Jakob groaned.

"Could you two not have sex on the beach right in front of us?" Jakob said.

Cage rolled his eyes. "Why are you two even here again?"

Ciara giggled and pushed aside her newly grown tree smack dab in the middle of the beach to give her more shade. "Because I'm planning your wedding next week. Everyone loves a destination wedding when it's at the beach."

That was all well and good, but he knew that he and Azy had to take advantage of every minute they had together. The pause in the war with the Black Dragon wouldn't last long.

Cage shifted into his dragon and snatched Azy up out of the water. She squealed and held onto him, although less and less each time he took her flying. He did a loop-de-loop and she clung a whole lot tighter, which he loved.

He flew her to a very special hideaway, especially for them. Before the crew began work on their new home. He had them make them a lovers' nest in some very tall, very hidden trees on his new property. There was only one way in or out – by air. So, they would not be disturbed.

Only one piece of furniture filled in the little treehouse. A big ole bed. They had used it extensively in the last few days. He couldn't get enough of her and she initiated sex with him more than he did, especially in the past few days.

He landed and tumbled them straight into the bed.

"Come over here and sit on my face, love. I've been hankering for your pussy all day." He pulled her back onto the bed, straddling him. It was his favorite place for her to be.

Her lashes lowered, and her honey eyes went golden, dark with her desire. "Well, I'm not going to say no to that."

He grabbed her ass and pulled her toward him. "I didn't think you would."

Cage lifted her up and over him so her pussy was right where he wanted it to be. Where he could see and taste her. He would never tire of looking at her folds, dripping for him, or her flavor.

That salty sweet flavor of her was the best, most erotic flavor in the world.

He spread her open and licked her clit, pressing his tongue hard against it, exactly as she liked. But his favorite thing to do was to suck it like a ripe piece of fruit. That drove her insane.

Azy moaned and ground against him. God, he loved that sound. He gripped her hips in his hands and held her body tight. With one hand he cupped her ass and then found her tight asshole. He massaged it with the tip of his finger and gently pushed through the tight ring of muscles. She cried out his name and gushed her juices into his mouth.

He was being greedy and pushing her to climax as fast as he could because his cock was aching to be inside of her.

He pumped his finger in and out, sucked rhythmically on her clit, and then smacked her ass. She came in his mouth, shuddering and calling his name.

He didn't let up for a second and she was so sensitive, it didn't take him long to make her come. Twice more.

"Your tongue should be a registered weapon. My god," she panted. "Who needs a vibrator, when I've got you?"

"Dirty girl. Are you hinting at what you'd like me to do to you?"

"Not at all. Why, does that give you ideas?"

Oh so many.

Cage reached into the little basket beside the bed and pulled out a hot pink vibrating butt plug. One of his favorite things to do was to watch her masturbate while he slid this into her ass.

Ass play drove her wild. Today, they would do more than play. "Turn around so I can put this in your luscious ass, love. Then I want you to ride me."

He wet the vibrator in her own juices. There was more than enough to go around. Then he put the tip of it right at her little pucker.

"Ready, baby?"

"Mmm-hmm."

When she was panting again from the teasing he did with the plug, he slid it past the ring of muscle in her ass and inside of her.

"Oh, oh… oh god. Oh."

"That's it baby, you can take it. It's not that big and it's nice and wet."

She moaned the whole time. The vibrator went in the rest of the way and her muscles tightened, pulsing around it.

CAGE SAT on the bed and helped her find just the right position. He turned the vibe on and then put her on his lap, impaling her hot cunt with his cock. "Ride me, baby. I've been hard for you all day."

She wrapped her knees around his hips and sank down onto him. "Oh, God. Cage you feel so fucking big inside of me."

"I'm going to feel even bigger when I'm pumping my cock into your ass instead of this little toy."

"Fuck, you know how to romance a girl." She whimpered and moaned, driving him crazy with all her sexy little sounds.

Her tits were bouncing in front of his face. They were so ripe and lush. The nipples begged for him to suck them. He lapped at one and then the other.

"Ooh, yes. Do that some more. It feels so good. They've been so tender lately."

They had. In fact, her breasts looked bigger now. She had filled back out from her diet literally from hell. He loved watching her eat. She loved food and just to please her, he'd imported Portillo's hotdogs all the way from Chicago.

That had won him some serious brownie points and a particularly enthusiastic blow job.

Her lush curves drove him wild, all the dame time. They filled his mouth and his hands so perfectly. Now way he would ever get enough of her body, her sass, her love. Cage cupped her plump breast and sucked on her nipple hard like she wanted him to.

"Oh, fuck. I'm going to come again if you keep doing that."

He kept doing that.

She grabbed onto his shoulders and dug her nails into him. "Cage, Cage. Fuck, yes. I'm coming."

It took everything in him not to explode right along with her. But, he'd been looking forward to fucking her ass for a long time. Now that he had her nice and relaxed, he was going to take her and claim her in the only way he hadn't yet.

He laid her out on the bed and grabbed a bottle of locally made coconut oil from the basket. He spread some on her back and massaged her muscles there.

"Mmm. That feels so good."

He took his time, kneading her back and then her plump ass. If he didn't cool his own jets first, he wouldn't get to savor fucking her. The vibrator was still in her tight ass. He turned it off and then grabbed the end of it and gave a little twist, reawakening her senses there.

"Oh. Mmm." She groaned. "Why does that feel so good?"

"Because you're nice and relaxed now. You're going to enjoy this as much as I am."

He pulled the vibrator out of her ass and replaced it with his fingers, full of the oil. He massaged the tight ring, opening her more, preparing her body so she would get only pleasure out of their joining.

That's what he wanted for her always.

When she began wriggling and moaning at his ministrations, panting and pushing back against him, he withdrew his fingers and gave her a light swat on her delicious ass, then followed it up with a kiss right in the small of her back.

"Are you ready, love?

He waited for her to answer and when she said gripped the sheets and moaned out her yes, his cock was poised and ready to go. She threw her hair back and put her knees underneath herself, angling her ass up.

"Oh, hell, yes. That's it, Azy. Give me your sweet, sweet ass."

"I need you Cage. Now."

He pushed the head of his cock past the tight ring of muscles, gritting his teeth, trying his best to take her slow.

Azy panted hard and swallowed. "More. I want to feel you all the way inside of me."

He went deeper in to her, until he was fully-seated. He held his breath and squeezed the very base of his cock to keep from coming right then and there. This would be good for both of them.

Cage gripped her hips with his hands and slowly withdrew almost all the way again. He took long deep thrusts until the rhythm he set pushed them both to the edge faster than he'd wanted too.

"Put your hand between your legs and finger your clit," he growled out. He was losing his control and Azy wasn't ready to come yet.

She did as he told her, and it created ripples that squeezed his cock inside of her. He was done being gentle, and fucked her ass fast and hard now, groaning out her name, losing himself in her completely.

"Oh. Please...Cage. It's too much. I can't..." Her channel clenched around him so tight that he couldn't hold back any longer either, and they came together.

He collapsed over her on the bed and then rolled, wrapping her in his arms, caressing her body. They drifted together in the afterglow of their intense love-making. When he could actually form coherent words again he whispered sweet and sensual words of love into her ear.

She did the same and they relaxed into to each other, enjoying being wrapped up together in their own little world.

His hands wandered along her hips, into that dip at her waist he adored, and up her rib cage. She guided his touch to her breasts, and he circled the soft skin of her areolas, teasing her until her nipples grew hard again.

"Babe. Your tits are bigger, aren't they? Like they're growing."

She moved his hands from her breasts to her stomach. "That's not the only thing that's growing."

His fingers danced over her abdomen. It was rounder than before.

Gulp. "Uh. Love. Either you're hungry or an alien has invaded your stomach because I just felt something move."

"Cage. How do you feel about dragon babies?"

Holy.

Shit.

Cage flipped her and crawled over her body. He stared straight at her stomach, narrowing his eyes and opening all of his senses. Oh, yes. He could scent it now. He'd been so focused on having down and dirty sex with her, he hadn't noticed the new life growing inside of her.

"You're pregnant."

"I know." She grinned up at him.

"Why didn't you tell me?"

"I just did. I only figured it out this morning. I don't know how long dragon or mermaid gestation is, but it seems they grow faster than humans. I feel like I'm way bigger than I should be at this point."

"Well, that's because there are two of them in there."

"What?"

He laughed. "Yep. I can scent two distinct new lives."

"I love you. You're changing diapers."

He would do that and so much more. Anything and everything for her and their children.

Because he was in love with his very own mermaid.

NEED MORE curvy girls getting their happy ever afters?

Go here http://geni.us/GiveMeCurvyConnection

You'll get book release news, contests and giveaways, and exclusive previews and excerpts. I'll send you another curvy girl romance book just to say thanks! You can even join my review team and get the next book before it's even released.

KEEP READING for a letter from me, the author, for you, the reader, about what's coming next in the Dragons Love Curves series.

WHO LOVES DRAGONS?

A letter from the Author

Dear reader,

I hope you loved reading this adventure in the Dragons Love Curves series with Cage and Azynsa as much as I loved writing it!

The dragons and their mates have a lot more adventures coming your way. So many questions to be answered.

I've got some fun surprises coming in the next books in the Dragons Love Curves series, so be sure to follow me on Amazon, Bookbub, Facebook, or my Curvy Connection to find out what happens next (hint: dragon babies are coming, and a certain succubus is going to put up quite the fight when her mates come to claim her.)

Stay tuned to get your fix of sexy dragon shifters giving their mates happy ever afters (and happy endings! Lol)

If you haven't read the book that started it all, check out *Chase Me* where you'll get to read about Jakob Zeleny, the Green Dragon Wyvern, and his mate Ciara's love adventure. You can binge read dragon shifters and their curvy mates for days!

I'd love if you left a review for this story. I really appreciate you telling other readers what you thought.

Even if you're not sure what to say – it can be as simple as – "Loved this story." or "Hooray for curvy girls and dragons." Just one sentence will do a lot.

Want to be the first to know when the next book comes out (plus get cool exclusive content from me!)? Sign up for my Curvy Connection mailing list. Go here http://geni.us/GiveMeCurvyConnection

Find me at www.AidyAward.com or on Facebook, Twitter, Instagram, or follow me on BookBub.

Kisses,

~Aidy

Dragons Love Curves

Chase Me

Tease Me

Bite Me

Cage Me

Baby Me

More Dragons coming soon~

Fated for Curves

A Curvy Girl Sci-fi Romance Series

set in Magic, New Mexico.

A Touch of Fate

A Tangled Fate

A Twist of Fate

More Fated for Curves stories coming soon~

The Curvy Love Series

Curvy Diversion

Curvy Temptation

Curvy Persuasion

Curvy Domination (coming soon)

The Curvy Seduction Saga

Rebound

Rebellion

Reignite

ABOUT THE AUTHOR

Aidy Award is a curvy girl who kind of has a thing for stormtroopers. She's also the author of the popular Curvy Love series and the hot new Dragons Love Curves series.

She writes curvy girl erotic romance, about real love, and dirty fun, with happy ever afters because every woman deserves great sex and even better romance, no matter her size, shape, or what the scale says.

Read the delicious tales of hot heroes and curvy heroines come to life under the covers and between the pages of Aidy's books.

Then let her know because she really does want to hear from her readers.

Connect with Aidy on her website. www.AidyAward.com get her Curvy Connection, and join her Facebook Group - Aidy's Amazeballs.

16865544R00106

Printed in Great Britain
by Amazon